THIS TOO
SHALL *Pass*

THIS TOO SHALL Pass

EDWARD VAUGHN

iUniverse, Inc.
Bloomington

This Too Shall Pass

iUniverse books may be ordered through booksellers or by contacting:

iUniverse
1663 Liberty Drive
Bloomington, IN 47403
www.iuniverse.com
1-800-Authors (1-800-288-4677)

ISBN: 978-1-4759-1024-7 (sc)
ISBN: 978-1-4759-1025-4 (hc)
ISBN: 978-1-4759-1108-4 (ebk)

Printed in the United States of America

iUniverse rev. date: 03/30/2012

No matter what you have,
Don't envy those you meet.
It's all the same;
It's in the game
Of the bitter and the sweet.

(From the beautiful old song,
The Bluebird of Happiness.)

CHAPTER ONE

On a clear and chilly early December afternoon in the college town of Chapel Hill, North Carolina, the annual football game between two major Atlantic Coast Conference college teams, the University of North Carolina Tar Heels and the Duke University Blue Devils, was in progress at the Tar Heels' Keenan Stadium. As with all competitive sports events between these two traditional old rivals, their school's pride was on the line . . . especially for this game, since the winner would also clinch the Atlantic Coast Conference championship. Both teams had been giving it their all, and at the end of the first half of the hard fought game the score was tied at seven-seven.

After both teams had left the playing field and returned to their respective locker rooms for the half-time break, the overflow crowd rose to their feet with loud cheers and a thundering applause as a University of North Carolina player wearing number 14 jogged onto the football field, giving a friendly waive to the cheering crowd, and then stood at the fifty yard line alongside his parents and the President of the University of North Carolina.

The President's voice boomed out over the stadium's public address system: "Mr. James Wilson McDonald the third, during your years as a student at the University of North Carolina, you have distinguished yourself through your many noteworthy accomplishments and exceptional personal qualities. These include your outstanding athletic ability, sterling scholastic record, excellent leadership, strong moral character, and willingness to help many of the less fortunate members of our community.

Every year, a student athlete is selected by the University's Board of Trustees to receive a special honor. For your many achievements and for the splendid example which you have set for our future student athletes to follow, it is now my pleasure on behalf of our Board of Trustees to present you with this plaque naming you as *The University of North Carolina's Student Athlete of the Year.*" The President handed the young man the plaque, shook his hand, and then handed him the microphone to respond.

"Mr. President, I sincerely thank you and the Board of Trustees for bestowing such a special honor upon me, sir. I am deeply grateful to the University for providing me with a wonderful education and the many other memorable experiences I've enjoyed during the time I've been here at this great university. I shall always remember my years as a Tar Heel as some of the most rewarding of my life.

I'm also grateful to the many that have helped me reach this point in my life, especially our dear Lord, my beloved mother and father, my learned professors, my fraternity brothers, my many friends and teammates, and our fabulous Tar Heel football fans. From the bottom of my heart, my deepest thanks to you all.

Now, if you good folks will please excuse me, I've got to hustle on back to the locker room with my team mates and get ready to put a good whipping on those dadgummed pesky old Duke Blue Devils in the next half, and bring the ACC championship to Chapel Hill!"

He gave his mother and father a warm hug, shook the President's hand again; then, with the award plaque tucked under his arm, waved to the crowd with a wide smile as he jogged off the field and back to the North Carolina Tar Heels' locker room.

As his very proud parents returned to their seats with happy tears glistening on the cheeks of their smiling faces, the crowd resumed its admiration of the young football star with another standing, thundering round of applause and cheers.

When the nail-biting tied second half was nearly over, Duke scored a field goal with only one minute left on the play clock. It appeared to be a certain victory for the Blue Devils when North Carolina had the ball on their forty-eight yard line with fourth down and six and only ten seconds left in the game. The Duke fans were high-fiving each other over what seemed to be a certain victory for them, and the glum Tar Heel fans were beginning to exit from the stadium.

Wilson knew the odds weighed heavily against him, but he still hadn't given up. He drew back to pass and was quickly surrounded by several aggressive Blue Devil lineman who were about to sack him. Then, with incredulous determination, he rapidly powered past them and the Duke secondary for fifty-two yards and a touchdown, winning the game and the Atlantic Coast Conference championship for the Tar Heels, 14-10. There was dancing in the streets that night in Chapel Hill! This was a game that would be remembered and talked about by the Tar Heel fans for years to come!

*   *   *

James Wilson McDonald, III, known to his friends, family, and colleagues as "Wilson," had experienced the kinds of successes during his college years and throughout his young life for which many men would gladly die!

These successes include being an outstanding quarterback on the University of North Carolina Tar Heels football team, where he was selected for the first-string All-Atlantic Coast Conference and second-string All-American teams; serving as president of his Alpha Tau Omega college fraternity and vice president of the Student Body, and graduating *summa cum laude* with a bachelor of Arts degree in International Economics and a minor in Theology.

Tall at six-four with a solid athletic physique, Wilson had "Carolina blue" eyes, thick sandy brown hair, and pearly white teeth that accentuated his movie-star handsome face. He was always charming, well-spoken, outgoing, and commanded the immediate admiration of just about everyone he met, although he would sometimes unintentionally stir up feelings of inferiority and jealousy with some men, and nearly every woman who met him viewed him as the proverbial knight in shining armor.

After his graduation from the University of North Carolina, Wilson was a first-round National Football League draft pick and offered a contract to play professional football for the Washington Redskins. The contract included a large signing bonus and a substantial starting annual salary of almost a million dollars. This opportunity would have been a dream-come-true for most men!

However, to the shocked surprise of his many friends and his parents, Wilson made the decision to put his plans of pursuing a professional football career on hold and, instead, chose to enlist in the Army to help fight in the war that was raging in the Middle East where a close cousin, Warren McDonald, was still serving and two of his former high school teammates had recently lost their lives in battle. He considered this to be a moral obligation on his part to honor their sacrifices by serving his country, and signed up for a three-year enlistment.

After completing his basic and advanced individual training as a Private at Fort Jackson, South Carolina, Wilson was selected to attend the Army's Infantry Officer Candidate School at Fort Benning, Georgia. He graduated from the six months of rigorous training at the top of his class and was commissioned as a Second Lieutenant of infantry.

He then completed the physically demanding Ranger and Airborne training with ease, and was assigned to the 505th Parachute Infantry Regiment of the 82nd Airborne Division at Fort Bragg, North Carolina as an infantry platoon leader. Shortly after reporting for duty at Fort Bragg, he was deployed to the Middle East with his unit that had the mission of ejecting the Iraqi Army from the small country of Kuwait.

During a major combat skirmish on the Kuwait-Iraq border, Wilson was seriously wounded in the shoulder by a large rocket grenade fragment that nearly ripped his rotator cuff muscle to shreds while attempting to rescue one of the soldiers in his platoon, PFC Deshawn Jackson, who had been pinned down by enemy fire, was badly wounded, and near death. Fortunately, PFC Jackson's life was saved, and Wilson was awarded the Silver Star medal for his heroism and the Purple Heart medal for his wound.

Although PFC Jackson's life was saved, he lost a leg and was subsequently medically discharged from the service. He then went on to graduate from North Carolina State University with a doctoral degree in mathematics, and become a professor of mathematics at Fayetteville State University. Dr. Jackson and his grateful family would remain in close touch with Wilson as one of their dearest friends for the rest of their lives.

Unfortunately, the damage caused by the wound to Wilson's shoulder permanently ended any chances for him to resume the professional football career he had planned to pursue after completing his military service. After going through several intensive surgeries and many weeks of rehabilitation at the Walter Reed Army Medical Center in Washington, he was finally medically discharged from the Army as a Captain.

Since playing professional football was no longer an option for Wilson, he decided to become a lawyer, with the long-range goal of someday serving as a judge. He applied for and was immediately accepted into the Harvard University School of Law.

*   *   *

As the only child of prominent and highly respected parents, Dr. and Mrs. James "Jimmy" Wilson McDonald, Jr. of Fayetteville, North Carolina, Wilson had been raised in his family's palatial home in Forest Lakes, one of the most upscale neighborhoods in town. This was a home his parents had built shortly after they were married and would live in for the remainder of their lives.

While in high school, Wilson had worked as a golf course maintenance worker and dining room waiter at the nearby Highland Country Club during his summer vacations and on weekends; served as a year-round volunteer helper at the Fayetteville Urban Ministries Food Bank; beautifully maintained his family's large yard; was an honor roll student; served as the senior acolyte and taught a Sunday School class for mentally challenged children at St. John's Episcopal

Church, and was a star athlete on the Terry Sanford High School's football, basketball, and baseball teams.

As financially well to do as Wilson's parents were, they always took special care to ensure that their son felt secure and loved, but they never spoiled or pampered him. They raised him in a careful and well-disciplined manner, and always encouraged him to be a strong, independent, responsible, positive-thinking, and morally straight gentleman.

As out of the ordinary as it was for the times, when young people had become so defiant towards traditional social and moral standards with their liberal use of vulgar language and sexual promiscuity that clean-living teenage virgins of either gender were virtually extinct, Wilson was committed to the old-fashioned conservative moral standards his parents had firmly instilled in him . . . that all vulgar language was strictly forbidden, drinking alcoholic beverages wasn't allowed, and sexual intimacy was to be experienced only within the boundary of marriage.

Many attractive young girls in his high school class would often throw themselves at Wilson, viewing him as a prized catch, and he occasionally went out on friendly dates but never became too heavily involved with any particular girl. When he participated in such social events as his high school prom, he was always polite and gentlemanly, and never attempted to engage his dates in any form of sexual activity, drink alcohol, or use inappropriate language.

Because of his rigidly conservative personal standards, avoidance of vulgar talk, and abstinence from engaging in pre-marital sex or the use of alcohol, some of Wilson's jealous male peers of lesser intellect and character described him as an arrogant snob who believed he was superior to them.

Being the intelligent and calm-minded fellow he was, instead of becoming angry when these kinds of absurd criticisms would get back to him, Wilson would only laugh them off. He had a great sense of humor and had no trouble laughing at himself, and accepted criticism when it was warranted.

There was only one instance during his high school days when he completely unleashed his anger and engaged in an altercation with an immature and foul-talking fellow student when the young man called Wilson "a queer motherfucker" in front of his friends.

Wilson put an unmerciful beating on the foolish boy that left him with a smashed nose, the loss of two front teeth, and both of his eyes swollen shut and blackened. It took several of Wilson's friends and the school police officer to stop him from inflicting further damage on the boy. Fortunately, witnesses to the incident testified that Wilson was justified in his response to the verbal assault and no charges were filed against him. Word of the incident quickly spread around the school and that put a quick stop to any further aspersions on his character.

CHAPTER TWO

Wilson was born of the finest genetic stock. His highly-respected, athletic, and handsome father, Dr. Jimmy McDonald, was raised on a small dairy farm on the outskirts of Fayetteville, had served in the Army with the 101st Airborne Division as a combat medic in South Viet Nam, and then attended Duke University on a football scholarship where he was an outstanding running back. He earned a Bachelor of Science degree in Chemistry with honors, and later earned his medical degree from the Duke University School of Medicine.

After completing his internship and a residency in general surgery, Jimmy served as a general surgeon at the Cape Fear Valley Regional Medical Center in Fayetteville for twenty-five years and then retired from his surgical career at the early age of fifty-five.

After his retirement from Cape Fear, Jimmy did a lot of volunteer work with the CARE Clinic and several other local charitable organizations, served two terms on the Cumberland County Board of Commissioners and one term in the State House of Representatives, served as president of the Fayetteville Kiwanis and Rotary Clubs, and was a member of several major area corporations' boards of directors. Jimmy was one of the best known and respected men in Cumberland County.

However, as busy as his schedule was, at the very top of Jimmy's priorities in life was in being a devoted dad to his son, Wilson, and a loving and faithful husband to his wife, Elizabeth. He was an avid fisherman and hunter who often took Wilson with him on deep-sea fishing and hunting trips, taught him to play golf and tennis, and coached his Little League baseball and football teams. In short, his dad was always the hero and key role model in shaping Wilson's life and they were each other's best friend.

Wilson's very attractive and loving mother, Elizabeth, was a prominent socialite and an active member of the Cumberland County Republican Party; Daughters of the American Revolution; United Daughters of the Confederacy; Fayetteville Chapter of the Junior League; Fayetteville Council of the Arts; Vestry of the historic St. John's Episcopal Church, where she was also a soprano soloist in its choir, and the Highland Country Club where she was one of the Club's leading lady golfers.

A debutante, Elizabeth came from a prominent Greenville, North Carolina tobacco family and had just graduated from the exclusive St. Mary's College in Raleigh with a Bachelor of Arts degree in Classical Music when she met Jimmy one Sunday morning at the coffee social gathering after a church service at the Grace Episcopal Church in Raleigh.

Jimmy was near the completion of his internship at Raleigh's Wake County Memorial Hospital and scheduled to begin a residency in general surgery at the Cape Fear Valley Regional Medical Center in his hometown of Fayetteville.

It was true love at first sight for both of them, and Jimmy wasted no time in proposing to her. In defiance of the social protocols of their time, which traditionally placed six months to a year between an engagement announcement and the wedding, and much to her socially conscious family's chagrin, Jimmy and Elizabeth decided they couldn't wait that long, and were married by a Justice of the Peace in Dillon, South Carolina just four months after they first met.

They enjoyed a brief weekend honeymoon at the South of the Border Motel in Dillon, and their only child, Wilson, was born exactly nine months and three days after they were married . . . and they adored him!

While Wilson was away in his third year at Harvard Law School, a horrible tragedy occurred when his beloved parents were found murdered in an unsolved double homicide and robbery of their Fayetteville home.

As he beheld the bodies of his beloved mother and father lying in their side-by-side caskets at the Rogers and Breece Funeral Home in Fayetteville, Wilson felt totally devastated over the loss of the two most important people in his life. He recalled with sadness and deep gratitude that it was they who had given him life and their wonderful, loving guidance had made him who and what he was . . . and now they were gone from this life.

But the high personal moral standards and strong belief in an eternal life that they had instilled in him through his strong religious upbringing provided Wilson with the strength to help him cope with the otherwise unbearable grief created by this terribly painful loss.

Instead of viewing his parents as two lifeless bodies lying beside each other in caskets, he visualized them as now being the angels he knew they had become as he recalled the many wonderful and loving things they had done in raising him and the good times they shared together during their earthly life. Although he would sorely miss them, he had some comfort in knowing they were now enjoying their earned rewards and at peace with their Lord in a far better place.

*   *   *

While in his final year at Harvard University, Wilson proposed marriage on bended knee before the church congregation of the first steady and only serious girlfriend in his life, Rebecca "Becky" Dunlap. Becky was a very charming, intelligent, and attractive tall blonde who was a former high school and college classmate. She happily accepted his proposal and the beautiful five-karat flawless diamond engagement ring, set in platinum that had been his mother's.

Becky was also from Fayetteville and had been two years behind Wilson at Terry Sanford High School and at the University of North Carolina, but was from a far less prominent and stable family than his.

Her father, an alcoholic, drug addict, and frequently unemployed construction worker who often cheated on and beat her mother, had deserted the family when Becky was only three years old and was never heard from again.

Her uneducated, very poor, and chronically sick mother, Rhonda, had to rely on part-time waitressing at various local beer joints and "under the table" house cleaning jobs to supplement her food stamps, disability income, and other welfare benefits. She and her three children were barely able to survive in their small and dilapidated single-wide trailer in a run-down trailer park in Bonnie Doone, then one of the most deprived residential neighborhoods of Fayetteville.

The only pleasure Rhonda had been able to enjoy in her otherwise wretched and deprived life had been in satisfying a two pack a day addiction to cigarettes and a nightly bottle of cheap wine to anesthetize her sad and troubled mind. She suffered a miserable death at the age of forty-three due to complications from emphysema and cirrhosis of the liver.

Becky's only siblings were a brother, Samuel, who was twelve years older, and a sister, Roberta, who was eleven years older. Samuel was doing hard time at the North Carolina State Prison in Raleigh for illegal drug dealing and Roberta, who had become severely addicted to crack cocaine, dropped out of high school in the tenth grade after having two children by fathers unknown. The children were immediately placed for adoption and Roberta turned to prostitution for her survival. She was murdered by a "John" in a cheap downtown motel room just before reaching the age of nineteen.

Becky hadn't seen either of her siblings since she was seven years old, and was raised in a children's church group home in Fayetteville after her mother's death. Despite her family's many shortcomings and failures, Becky was determined that she would somehow create a better life for herself than the one in which she had been born. She was a strong, intelligent, and hard-driving achiever who always gave her all and excelled at nearly everything she undertook.

The opposite of her mother and siblings in nearly every way, Becky embraced the highest of personal and moral standards and was active in the First Christian Church of Fayetteville where she taught a children's Sunday school class, was the soloist in the church choir and, at the age of sixteen, became its youngest ever deacon.

She graduated at the top of her class at Terry Sanford High School two years after Wilson with a four-point plus grade point average, was an excellent athlete who excelled on the girls basketball, volleyball, and soccer teams, starred in the drama club's plays, and was the graduating Class Valedictorian and recipient of a full academic scholarship to the University of North Carolina at Chapel Hill.

While a student at Chapel Hill, Becky augmented her limited scholarship income by editing and typing term papers, and cleaning, sewing, and ironing for some of her more affluent and spoiled sorority sisters. She was selected as the Homecoming Queen; was Phi Beta Kappa; president of her Pi Beta Phi sorority; editor of the UNC student newspaper and yearbook; a regular volunteer at the Salvation Army Homeless Men's Shelter, and a star forward on the University's women's basketball team.

Becky was a sophomore and Wilson a senior when they first met while both were serving as volunteers at the Chapel Hill Salvation Army Homeless Men's Shelter and, as it had been with his parents when they first met many years before, it was true love at first sight for both of them!

Like Wilson, Becky also later graduated from UNC with highest academic honors, majoring in Elementary Education with a minor in Information Technology. She subsequently went on to earn her Master's degree in Elementary Education at the Methodist University in Fayetteville and began working as a fifth grade teacher at the Fayetteville Academy while Wilson was serving in the Army and, later, while he was away in law school.

Becky and Wilson would exchange lengthy love letters nearly every day, and spend all of their vacation times together. As much as they loved and wanted to be with each other, being the practical-minded and responsible people they were, they decided it would be best for them to wait until after Wilson graduated from law school before they "tied the knot."

*   *   *

After Wilson graduated from Harvard Law School with honors, he and Becky, who were both firmly committed to each other, still virgins by choice, and in their late twenties, were married in an elegant, royal type wedding at the First Christian Church in Fayetteville. A magnificent reception at the Highland Country Club followed the wedding ceremony and was in attendance by nearly everyone of importance in Cumberland County. It was unquestionably the social event of the year in Fayetteville society.

During their fairy tale like honeymoon on a ten-day cruise on a Carnival Cruise ship in the Caribbean, they spent many happy hours together in their luxurious cabin enjoying their first ever intimate sexual experiences. This exciting new part of their relationship was initially a little awkward for these two neophyte virgins; but by the time they returned from their cruise back to the port of Tampa, Florida, they had become quite proficient in the delightful art of lovemaking.

Wilson and Becky immediately went to work in building a family. She eagerly looked forward to becoming an outstanding and devoted wife and mother like hers hadn't been, and he in becoming a super and loving husband and father like his had been. Later, while in waiting for the birth of her first child, Becky published a series of children's books which quickly became profitable best sellers.

Wilson's first job after graduating from law school was a one-year apprenticeship as the law clerk for a Federal District Court judge in Wilmington, North Carolina. After the completion of his apprenticeship with the Federal Judge, he was offered and accepted a position as a Securities and Exchange compliance attorney in the legal department of Barnett, Breckenridge, and Company, Inc., on Wall Street in New York City, one of the most prestigious international institutional securities firms in the world.

In just two years, he was promoted to serve as the General Counsel of the large firm, and was the youngest person in the history of the over one-hundred-year-old company to hold that position.

Becky and Wilson were quickly blessed with four lovely daughters: Elizabeth, Taylor, Sarah, and Lauren, who were nearly spitting images of their mother and had been born about one year apart. All four girls were very attractive, loving, bright, clean-living, well-behaved, and would become honor roll students.

Their oldest daughter, Elizabeth, was a natural athlete who excelled in several sports; followed by Taylor who was a gifted artist and writer; Sarah, a talented little actress with a great sense of humor for her young age, and little Lauren, being the youngest, was a cute little "love bug" who captured everyone's hearts with her ballet dancing and sweet singing voice.

The McDonald's resided in a large, elegant six bedroom mansion they had built on a three-acre wooded lot which backed into a large county park and had a large in-the-ground swimming pool and tennis court in a gated section of the elite and affluent New York City bedroom community of Saddle River, New Jersey. They also owned a rustic vacation home on Lake Lure in the North Carolina Mountains near Rutherfordton, and a beautiful beachfront home on Topsail Island, North Carolina.

By the time Wilson was forty-one years old, through receiving a substantial inheritance of about twenty million dollars from his deceased parents' estate, along with some brilliant investing on his part, he and Becky had acquired a financial net worth of just over one hundred million dollars. He also enjoyed a large six-figured salary as the General Counsel of his firm, and the family income was further supplemented by the substantial royalties that Becky earned from the sale of her popular series of children's books.

By most people's standards, Wilson and Becky had it "made in the shade," but they never took their many blessings for granted and gave daily prayers of thanks to their Lord for providing them.

CHAPTER THREE

At a little after midnight just a few days before Christmas and during an unusually heavy snowstorm, a large late model black Mercedes-Benz sedan bearing a New Jersey license plate moved slowly along a snow-covered and empty Wall Street in New York City's financial district. After slowly cruising around the area for several minutes, the automobile suddenly turned into a narrow alleyway located behind a large office building at 44 Wall Street, stopped, and the headlights were switched off.

The driver quickly got out of the car and threw open the trunk; then dragged a large blanket-wrapped bundle out and propped it up against a brick wall in the alley. A corner of the blanket flipped open and the badly beaten and bloody face of a young African-American woman was exposed, and a nearly empty bottle of Scotch whiskey was wedged into her stiffened, cold hand. The driver then jumped back into the car and headed north on Manhattan's West Side Highway, disappearing into the dark and miserable winter night.

*   *   *

Earlier that evening, two days before their children's school Christmas vacation was to begin, Wilson, Becky, and their three other daughters had watched their oldest daughter, fifteen-year-old Elizabeth, play in her high school girls' basketball game where she scored the game winning goal with a three point jump shot in the last two seconds of play, defeating their arch-rival, nearby Pascack Hills High School, by one point!

After the exciting, nip and tuck basketball game was over, the McDonald family celebrated Elizabeth's athletic achievement together over a nice dinner at the posh Saddle River Country Club. On their way back home, they picked up a large and beautifully shaped cedar Christmas tree at the annual Pascack Valley Lions Club's fundraising sale to take home and decorate.

Following an enjoyable evening of laughter and fun, singing Christmas carols, nibbling on freshly baked Christmas cookies and sipping warm apple cider while they decorated their beautiful Christmas tree, the McDonald family knelt together in a semi-circle around the tree and held hands while they said their nightly prayers of thanksgiving for their many blessings . . . then everyone retired to their bedrooms for the evening.

In the king-sized bed of their magnificently decorated large upstairs master bedroom, Becky and Wilson enjoyed a warm, exciting, and deeply satisfying lovemaking session . . . an almost nightly event for them.

These two lovebirds had become highly prolific and proficient lovers during their sixteen years of a wonderful marriage, and would humorously refer to their frequent lovemaking sessions as their "favorite sleeping pill." They both then fell into a deep and relaxing sleep at a little after eleven o'clock.

Shortly after midnight, the front doorbell of their home began ringing non-stop and awakened Wilson from his deep sleep. Annoyed, he sat up in the bed and muttered aloud, "Who in the world could that be at our front door this late at night and why the heck do they keep on ringing the doorbell like that?"

Becky mumbled, "Honey, please hurry and go find who it is before they wake up the children."

Wilson quickly jumped out of bed, donned a terrycloth bathrobe and bedroom shoes, and slipped a .38 caliber revolver in his pocket; then cautiously tip-toed down the stairs to the front door.

When he peered through the door's peephole, he was shocked to see many flashing lights coming from the domes of several police cars that were lined up in his driveway and reflecting their bright red and blue colors across the snow-covered front yard. A portly, grim-faced, man wearing a tan trench coat and hat stood on the front porch. Flanked on each side of the plain clothed man were two uniformed Bergen County Sheriff's Department deputies with their pistols drawn and raised at the ready.

Stunned by what he saw, he thought, *what in heaven's name could this be?* He slowly cracked open the front door and the heavy-set plain clothed man quickly barged into the large foyer. He flashed a gold Bergen County detective's badge in Wilson's face and sternly asked him, "Are you Mr. James Wilson McDonald, the third?"

"Yes sir, I am, and what seems to be the problem here, officer?"

"Mr. McDonald, I'm Lieutenant Anthony Marciano, a homicide detective with the Bergen County Sheriff's Department, and I have a warrant for your arrest which charges you with the murder of Miss Yolanda Lee Walker of New York City."

He pulled a small laminated 3x5 card from his coat pocket and read aloud from it. "Before you say anything, sir, it is my duty to advise you of your rights. You have the right to remain silent and have an attorney present when you are questioned, and anything you say from this point on may be used against you in a court of law. If you can't afford an attorney, one will be provided for you. Do you understand your rights, Mr. McDonald?"

"What in the world are you talking about?" a shocked Wilson asked. "Yolanda Walker is my administrative assistant and she left on a vacation trip to the Bahamas with her fiancée for the Christmas holidays a couple of days ago. And of course I understand my Miranda rights. I happen to be an attorney, but I'm sure as heck not a murderer. This is totally crazy! I saw her just a couple of days ago at my office and she was perfectly fine. Are you sure you're talking about my administrative assistant, Yolanda Walker?"

"Yes sir, I'm absolutely certain of it. Her body was identified by her parents at the Medical Examiner's office in New York City early yesterday morning. The New York City District Attorney has good reason to believe that you are the one who murdered her and that's why we're here to arrest and take you into custody."

As Wilson and the detective, surrounded by the four armed deputies, were standing in the entrance foyer, Becky came down the stairs, sleepy-eyed and clutching her bathrobe. She asked, "What in the world is going on here so late at night with all this noise, honey, and who are all of these people?"

Wilson shrugged his shoulders in frustration. "This gentleman is a Bergen County detective, and he just advised me that Yolanda Walker, my legal assistant at the office, has been found dead and I've been charged with her murder."

Startled by what Wilson said, Becky frowned and angrily snapped back, "That's impossible and completely ridiculous, and I don't believe a word of it! This has got to be somebody's idea of a sick practical joke, and I don't find it one darned bit funny!"

Lieutenant Marciano grimly replied, "I'm afraid it's not a joke, ma'am; it's very real and quite serious, so please step aside while I do what I must. Mr. McDonald, please kneel down and place your hands on top of your head with your fingers interlocked while I search you for weapons; then I'll apply handcuffs and take you to the Department Headquarters in Hackensack for questioning. Afterwards, you will be extradited over to the New York City authorities later today to be formally charged."

With Becky standing in the front doorway, still shocked over what was happening and crying her eyes out, a handcuffed Wilson, attired only in his bathrobe and bedroom shoes and sans his pistol, was placed into the back seat of a Deputy Sheriff's cruiser. They then traveled down the snow-covered road in the middle of an escort convoy of several other Sheriff's Department cruisers with their red and blue dome lights flashing, and headed for the Sheriff's Department headquarters in the Bergen County town seat of Hackensack.

After they arrived at the department headquarters at a little after one a.m., Wilson was immediately taken into the interrogation room where his handcuffs were removed and he was directed to sit in a chair opposite Lieutenant Marciano and a stenographer.

Lieutenant Marciano again advised Wilson of his Miranda rights, told him their conversation was being transcribed and recorded on videotape, and asked if he wanted to have an attorney present during his questioning.

Still clad in only his bathrobe and bedroom slippers, an annoyed and tired Wilson, who almost never showed his anger or used expletives, replied in an uncharacteristically hostile manner, "Hell no! I don't need a damned lawyer because I've done nothing wrong and have absolutely nothing to hide, so please go ahead with your questions, Lieutenant, and let's get this damned ridiculous thing over with as soon as possible. I have to be at my office later today to do a lot of work in preparation for a very important meeting in New York City with our firm's Board of Directors in just a couple of days after Christmas."

"Mr. McDonald, would you tell me where you were the day before last?"

"Yes sir. It was supposed to be my day off, but I spent most of it at my office working on the presentation I just mentioned that I'm scheduled to provide for our firm's Board of Directors later in the week. Right after I finish making the presentation, my family and I have plans to go away for a week's Christmas and New Year's vacation trip down to our place in the mountains of North Carolina and then visit with our friends and family back in our hometown of Fayetteville.

When I was finished with my work at the office, I took the IRT subway uptown to the Pennsylvania Railroad Station and then headed directly home to New Jersey on the Amtrak commuter train. My wife and children met me at the Westwood AmTrack train station and can verify this."

"Was Miss Yolanda Walker at your office with you during the time while you were there?"

"Yes sir, she was there but for only a little while. She was helping me set up our company's conference room for a Power Point presentation that I'm scheduled to give at next week's Board meeting. She had to leave the office at about two-thirty in the afternoon because she was scheduled to fly out of LaGuardia Airport with her fiancée on a Christmas vacation trip to the Bahamas later that afternoon. Approximately a couple of hours after Miss Walker left the office, I also left and went directly home."

"Did you and Miss Walker consume any alcoholic beverages during the time the two of you were together that day, Mr. McDonald?"

"No, sir, I don't drink alcohol at all—never have and never will—and I'm almost certain that Miss Walker would never touch the nasty stuff either."

"Were you and Miss Walker having other than a business relationship with each other?"

Wilson indignantly asked, "Would you please explain to me what you mean by that question, Detective?"

Marciano leaned forward and said with a smirking grin, "Come on now Mr. McDonald, and let's not play naïve games with each other. I think you know exactly what I mean . . . like were you romantically or sexually involved with her in any way?"

Wilson angrily replied, "Absolutely not, and I deeply resent anyone who would even suggest that I would do such a thing! I adore my dear wife, have always been faithful to her, and would never even think of violating our marriage vows with anyone for any reason, especially with someone who worked for me and is nearly half my age.

I liked and respected Miss Walker very much because she was a very nice young lady and an excellent administrative assistant, but our relationship was strictly business and nothing else. Whoever would say otherwise is either totally crazy or is trying to tie me into something I didn't do for whatever their reason."

"Are you completely certain of that, Mr. McDonald?"

"Listen, Lieutenant Marciano. I understand that you're doing your job and I really do want to be cooperative with you, because I'm very saddened to hear of Miss Walker's death and also want justice for her and her family, but I deeply resent your implication that I would do such a horrible thing.

If you have something concrete to support your obviously incorrect suspicion of me, please let me know what it might be and I'll try my best to clear it up for you; otherwise, I may be forced to obtain legal counsel. This whole thing is absolutely ridiculous and unless you can give me a reason why I should continue with this absurd conversation I prefer not to discuss it any further."

"That's entirely up to you, Mr. McDonald, but we have good reasons to believe that you had the means, opportunity, and motive to murder Miss Yolanda Walker, the details of which I'm not at liberty to share with you at this time. So, if you have nothing further to say to me now, this questioning session is over with as far as I'm concerned.

You may contact your lawyer if you wish, but we're going to keep you here in custody pending your being extradited to New York City later today where you will be formally charged with murder in the first degree."

Wilson placed a phone call to the home of his attorney friend, neighbor, and fellow Kiwanis Club member, Mark Horowitz, awakening him at three a.m. and described his situation. Mark assured him that he would contact the New York City District Attorney, Conrad Stevens, first thing later in the morning to find out what he could about the situation and try to negotiate bail; but said it could take at least a few days, maybe even weeks, to work all of that out.

He was then put through a humiliating body strip search by a corrections officer, given an orange prison jump suit and shower shoes to wear, and locked up in a cell which contained only a small cot, toilet, and sink, where he would remain until he would be transferred to the New York City Detention Center in Manhattan later that day.

Throughout the morning, all of the area radio and television stations were abuzz with non-stop reports of the story of the murder, and the front page of the morning's edition of *The Bergen Record* showed a large photograph of Wilson that had been taken from the newspaper's files when he was honored three months earlier as the Saddle River Kiwanis Club's Man of the Year, with the following story:

Local Attorney Charged With Secretary's Murder!

The District Attorney of New York City, Conrad Stevens, early today announced that James Wilson McDonald, III, 42, of Saddle River, New Jersey was arrested last night at his home and will be charged with the first-degree murder of Miss Yolanda Lee Walker, 21, of the Borough of Queens in New York City.

McDonald is General Counsel for the Wall Street international institutional brokerage firm of Barnett, Breckenridge and Company in New York City where Miss Walker had served as his administrative assistant for the past two years. Her body was discovered early yesterday morning wrapped in a blanket and propped against a wall in an alley behind an office building at 44 Wall Street in New York City.

According to his preliminary findings, the New York City Medical Examiner, Dr. Phillip Abramson, reported that Miss Walker had been severely beaten and appeared to have consumed a large amount of alcohol prior to her death.

McDonald's attorney, Mark Horowitz, also of Saddle River, was contacted and stated that his client is completely innocent of these groundless charges, and would probably be immediately released when all the facts in this case surface. Calls to the McDonald home were not returned. A trial date will be set for McDonald after his extradition from New Jersey to New York City, which is scheduled for later today.

*   *   *

As Wilson sat alone on a cot in the small jail cell, he searched his brain for any possible reason why he would be accused of murdering Yolanda. When he last saw her just a couple of days ago she was happy and excited about her vacation plans to spend the Christmas holidays in the Bahamas with her long-time boyfriend and recently announced fiancée, Tyrone Morris.

He thought, *Alcohol? No way with Yolanda. She was a very spiritual-minded and clean-living young woman who had frequently expressed her abhorrence towards alcohol and drugs. None of this makes any sense at all!*

Wilson had hired Yolanda to serve as his principal administrative assistant right after she graduated with honors from the Queens County Community College, where she had earned an Associate of Arts degree in Paralegal Administration.

Wilson further thought *I just can't understand how in the world anyone could even suspect that Yolanda and I could have been having an illicit affair. She was one absolutely beautiful and very smart young woman, for sure, but I had no personal interest at all in her, and that wasn't just because of our work relationship or ethnic and age differences. Everyone who knows me must know that I've always been totally loyal to my wife and my family, and would never even think of cheating on them with anyone for any reason. This is a completely crazy nightmare and makes no sense at all!*

He tried to recall any time that he and Yolanda might have been together outside of the office. He remembered having taken her to lunch at nearby Delmonico's Restaurant on the day after he hired her, the year before last, and a couple of months ago when he drove her from the office in his car to her parents' home in Queens when she became ill with the flu. He was certain that those were the only times they had ever been together outside of the office. *What in the world is happening here and why? I've done nothing wrong . . . this is completely insane!*

Chapter Four

After a sleepless night of sitting alone on the cot in his cell, at 10:30 a.m. a tall and heavy-set female corrections officer appeared at the cell door and said, "Inmate McDonald, you have two visitors here to see you; it's your lawyer and your wife, so place your hands through the slot on the cell door so I can apply these handcuffs, then I'll place chains on your legs and lead you to them."

Wilson complied with the officer's directions, was handcuffed and his ankles chained; and then led shuffling down the hallway on a long chain like a dog to a small conference room where Attorney Mark Horowitz and Becky, with teary and red puffy eyes, awaited him. Once inside the room, the corrections officer unlocked Wilson's handcuffs and removed his ankle chains.

After his restraints were removed, Becky rushed up to Wilson and attempted to give him a hug and kiss, but was abruptly stopped by the corrections officer who quickly stepped between them with her hands raised and sternly said, "Hey lady; there will be no physical contact between you and the prisoner or you will have to leave this facility right now. Do you understand me? You'll either comply with our visiting rules or else you're outta here!"

Becky withdrew from Wilson and glared her resentment at the officer. She had never been in such a personally degrading situation in her life and wanted to direct her anger at the officer, but knew she had no choice but to comply with the officer's order.

Wilson asked Becky, "How are our girls coping with this horrible nightmare, honey?"

Through choking tears, she sadly replied, "I suppose they're handling it as well as they could be expected to with their beloved daddy being publicly labeled as a murderer in the newspaper and seeing it aired on the local television channels all morning long.

We've been getting a steady stream of harassing phone calls from news reporters and a lot of very mean people saying hurtful and untrue things about you since six o'clock this morning and the girls have been crying their eyes out, even though I tried as best I could to explain to them that a mistake had been made and that it would soon be over and things would be alright. When our new maid, Betsy, heard about it on the news, she volunteered to come to our home early this morning to stay with the girls so I could come here with Mark to see you.

They were so terribly upset that they couldn't even go to school today, and all four of them have been constantly crying their eyes out all morning long. Lauren was supposed to dance and sing a solo in her class Christmas play on this last day of school before the Christmas holidays begin, but she was in no emotional shape for doing that or anything else."

Wilson replied, "Honey, I'm terribly sorry that you and our girls have had to go through so much humiliating embarrassment because of this ridiculous thing that's happening to me, which I still don't understand. But please let our precious girls know that I'm all right and I'll be coming back home to them as soon as this craziness is cleared up. I'm sure the New York District Attorney will soon realize this was a huge mistake and it should be resolved and all over with in the next day or so when the true facts surface."

Mark somberly injected, "Wilson, I hate to tell you, old buddy, but to be frank with you, it really doesn't look very good for you at this point and it's probably going to take us a good while longer than a few days before we'll even be able to get the entire picture. I spoke with the New York City District Attorney early this morning, and he has chosen to personally prosecute the case. He's a former classmate of mine from the Rutgers University Law School and filled me in on some of the details on which they based the charge.

It seems that a witness claims he saw someone driving a large fancy car, a black Mercedes-Benz sedan with a New Jersey license tag that apparently looked exactly like yours, traveling up and down Wall Street sometime between midnight and early morning the day before yesterday near the place where Miss Walker's body was found early the following morning.

The DA is convinced that you are the guy the witness claimed to have seen, based on his description of the automobile and some other information. He also told me a little about some of the other evidence he has and I'll be reviewing that in more detail at his office later on this afternoon."

"Good gosh, Mark, there are probably thousands of cars in the area that look exactly like mine, but mine was at home in the garage all night because I rode the commuter train in to New York every day this past week, like I usually do. Becky can testify to that, because she dropped me off at the train station early each morning this week and picked me up at the station early each evening.

What about Yolanda's boyfriend? Has anyone spoken with him? She told me she was supposed to be meeting him at LaGuardia Airport after she left the office for their flight to the Bahamas later that afternoon."

"Yep, he's already been thoroughly grilled by the cops in New York and is supposedly clean as a whistle with an airtight alibi. He claims that he left his workplace in Queens somewhere around three o'clock and waited for Yolanda at the airport from around four until after six when the Delta flight they were supposed to be on for the Bahamas had departed. Later that night, he said he called her parents who reported her to the police as missing, and her body was found behind a building near your office early on the following morning. And get this one, Wilson; her boyfriend also seems convinced that you are the one who murdered her!"

"What the heck could he base that ridiculous accusation on, Mark? I've never even met the guy and wouldn't recognize him if he walked into the room right now."

"According to the DA, her boyfriend told the New York Police investigators that he had recently received a tip on his cell phone from an anonymous male caller telling him that Yolanda was afraid of you because the two of you had been involved in a heavy love affair several months ago and she was trying to end it, but you wouldn't leave her alone and were angry at her for becoming engaged to him.

The DA also told me there were some pretty salacious e-mails found on your computer at the office from her to you that apparently supported that allegation, but they haven't been technically validated as yet." Upon hearing that, Becky broke into sobbing tears.

Wilson looked upward, put his hands on top of his head and loudly groaned, "This is absolutely insane! I don't recall ever getting any e-mails from her, especially anything of that ridiculous nature, and I rarely even used the computer in my office."

Mark asked, "Then what did you use for e-mails, internet, and business purposes at work?"

"I only used the lap top that I always carry back and forth with me from home each day for security reasons, and rarely used my office computer. This was also because I'm writing a murder mystery on my train trips back and forth from work that I hope to have published one day . . . that is, if I'm ever able to finish it. Did the investigators even bother to check Yolanda's computer to see if there were any e-mails on it from me to her?"

"Yes I'm sure they did, Wilson, and they have apparently not found anything yet, but they'll probably want to seize your laptop soon, maybe even today, to check it out. I sure hope there's no possible connection that could be made between the murder mystery that you're writing and this terrible disaster."

"No Mark, there certainly isn't and I don't see how they could even connect my completely fictional story to this crazy situation in any way because it's totally unrelated. It's based on the unsolved murder of my dear parents, which took place back in North Carolina over seventeen years ago."

"I understand, old buddy, but you'd be surprised at how a clever prosecutor could put a negative spin on something like that and try to create a connection of it with Miss Walker's murder.

The investigators also found some romantic and pretty risqué greeting cards locked inside her desk drawer that appeared to be from you to her because they had your initials on them."

"That's completely insane, Mark. I'm sure a handwriting analyst would be able to prove that I never sent her such a thing. Obviously, somebody's trying to frame me for her murder! What's the next step for me in this nightmare?"

"You'll be extradited over to New York City later today to be arraigned. I'll petition for a bail bond hearing at your first appearance in Court."

"Good gosh, Mark, that could take several days or even weeks to happen. What do I tell the president of my firm? We have some very important business issues that have to be acted on by the Board of Directors in a couple of days that are time-sensitive and have to be resolved right away, like within a week."

"I'm sure your firm's president is already aware of your situation, Wilson, since it's been all over the news this morning, but I'll be glad to call him if you want and try to explain the situation to him. Do you have an assistant or someone else in the company who would be able to fill in for you at the Board meeting?"

"Yeah, I guess one of our executive vice presidents who worked closely with me on it would be able to handle it if they are available; but if they're not, then one of my assistants, probably Chester Franklin, will probably have to do it.

"Who is Chester Franklin?"

"He's our Chairman's nephew, but he's not that smart and will probably screw it up. Besides, I really don't trust him any further than I could throw this building. His unrealistic ambitions to replace me far exceed his abilities, and I'm sure the Chairman knows that better than anyone. How the idiot ever managed to get his law degree and pass the Bar exam has always absolutely amazed me.

I tried everything I could to help the little jerk shape up, but nothing ever seemed to work. Becky and I once even had him at our home for dinner a year ago and his behavior was nothing short of disgusting, and he used language that was more like that of a drunken sailor than that of a supposedly educated lawyer. I sure do hope the Chairman finds one of our other executives to make the presentation . . . anyone but that idiot, Chester, who'd probably embarrass us all and make us lose the deal that I've worked so hard on putting together for the past year.

This is an insane disaster that's about to screw up my and my family's whole life, not to mention the pain the Walker family must be suffering, and it could also screw up one of the biggest and most important initial public offering underwriting deals my firm has ever done!"

A corrections officer then walked into the room and coldly announced to everyone that their visiting time was up. Mark and a tearful Becky then left, and Wilson was led back to his jail cell, handcuffed and in leg chains.

*   *   *

Later that afternoon, Wilson was again handcuffed and chained, and placed into a Bergen County Sheriff's Department van along with two other prisoners; then driven through the continuing unusually heavy snow storm into New York City to the Manhattan House of Detention. Once he arrived there, he was again strip searched and placed into a large holding cell with three other men; a drug dealer, a street thug, and a pimp.

Lieutenant Marciano met with his New York Police Department counterpart, Lieutenant Matthew DeSessa, to turn Wilson over to the New York City authorities.

"Well Marciano, what's your impression of that guy, McDonald?" DeSessa asked.

"It's 'kinda hard to say yet, Matt, but I understand that he's apparently the only suspect you and the DA have to work with right now. He really didn't act like most guilty people do when we questioned him early this morning, but he's a damned lawyer and you know how those bastards are well trained to lie with a straight face. What's your DA saying as far as bonding him out goes?"

"The DA said he's gonna handle the prosecution himself and go to the mat on this one because it looks like it's gonna be a slam-dunk conviction for him. Between the eyewitness, e-mails, raunchy greeting cards, and the bottle of whiskey that was found on the victim with our suspect's fingerprints on it, he thinks he has more than enough evidence to get a sure-fire conviction. It looks to me like we've got the right guy, Marciano, and I'd bet my bottom dollar that McDonald's big shot, rich Republican ass is gonna spend the rest of his life in the slammer for this one."

CHAPTER FIVE

The New York City Medical Examiner completed the final details of the autopsy on Yolanda Walker's body later that afternoon and submitted his report to the New York City District Attorney's office. The report confirmed his initial finding that her death was the result of multiple cerebral hemorrhages and a severe loss of blood from having been struck in the head several times with a blunt object.

Abramson also noted in his autopsy report that, while his initial examination indicated slight traces of alcohol had been found on her lips and in her mouth, further examination revealed that no alcohol was found in her blood or stomach, nor did it appear that she had been sexually assaulted. The small amount of alcohol suggested that the murderer had tried to make it *appear* that Yolanda had consumed a large amount of the whiskey prior to killing her by pouring a lot of it into her mouth and placing the nearly empty bottle in her hands after killing her. He estimated that she had probably died sometime around midnight, two days ago.

Particularly damaging to Wilson was the Police Department's fingerprint technician's report which confirmed that the only fingerprints found on the bottle of Johnny Walker Blue Scotch whiskey found in Yolanda's hand clearly matched those of Wilson.

District Attorney Stevens was delighted with this information since he would be running for re-election in a few months. With this seemingly indisputable evidence, he was confident that he would get a slam-dunk conviction, and the high visibility case would be one of his easiest and most publicized cases ever, one which he decided to personally prosecute in order to enhance his campaign for re-election.

As the DA and his wife watched the coverage on television, he smiled and said to her, "Wow, Babe, this situation couldn't be better for us if I had planned it myself. Re-election, here I come after I get a sure-fire conviction and throw this rich Republican guy in the slammer for the rest of his frigging life . . . yippee!"

*   *   *

Christmas morning at the McDonald home was clearly the saddest day of the family's life. It was morosely quiet and none of the girls were the least bit interested in lighting the tree or opening their Christmas gifts. Becky tried her best to put on a cheerful and confident face, but each time she would try to say something encouraging to the girls, she would spontaneously break into sobbing tears herself

43

and they would quickly join in with her, huddling and crying together on the living room couch in front of the unlit family Christmas tree.

Becky finally stopped crying, wiped her eyes with the back of her hand, and dropped to her knees with her hands outstretched and raised. "Girls, let's all kneel down together and say a prayer for your Daddy and ask our dear heavenly Father to please end this nightmare and return him safely back home to us.

And let's stop with all the tears now girls, because you know your Daddy wouldn't want us to be sad and crying like this. He needs for us to be brave for him now." Holding hands, they knelt together and said a prayer for Wilson; then all five of them hugged together and spontaneously resumed their crying.

Through sobbing tears, Taylor asked Becky in a shaking voice, "Mommy, can we please go over to New York later today and try to see Daddy? And I vote that we don't open any of our Christmas gifts or even turn on our Christmas tree lights until he comes back home to us and we can all enjoy our Christmas celebration together as a family." The other girls echoed their agreement with Taylor's idea.

Becky hugged her and replied, "That's a really sweet idea, honey, and that's exactly what we will do. We'll see if we can all go together and see your Daddy later this morning after we go to the Christmas morning church service."

Becky called Mark Horowitz to ask where Wilson was being held and how they would go about visiting him.

Horowitz told her that Wilson was incarcerated in New York City at the Manhattan House of Detention, and gave her its location, visiting hours, and driving directions. He also told her he would contact the District Attorney's office to ensure that Becky and his daughters would be allowed to visit him, since he had previously been told that he wouldn't be allowed to have visits from family or friends for awhile.

Becky and the girls then dressed and went to the Holy Trinity Episcopal Church in the nearby town of Westwood for the early morning Christmas worship service, the church which Wilson and his family had attended for several years and where he was a key financial supporter, a member of the Vestry, and a licensed lay reader who frequently participated in the services.

When they entered the narthex of the beautiful old church, they received a nervously polite hug and Christmas greeting from one of the ushers who had been a good friend and neighbor of theirs for many years, and no mention was made of Wilson's situation. But as Becky and the girls entered their usual pew and knelt to pray, many eyes shifted toward them and muffled whispering could be heard throughout the church.

After the Christmas morning service was over and Becky and her daughters were preparing to leave, their priest, Reverend Ben Gerrardy, hugged each of them and whispered, "Keep praying and trusting in your faith, dear ones, because it will help to sustain you during these difficult times and I know that, like most of the unhappy

45

things that happen to us in life, this too shall pass. Keep your chins up and call me any time you need me. I'll try to go over to New York City to see him later, as soon as the roads are clear enough, and I'll get back to you with a report right afterwards."

The drive in to New York City was a real struggle for Becky, as the record heavy snow was continuing to fall all day long and challenged even the most experienced driver; but she and the girls were determined to go and see her beloved husband and their dear father in spite of the risk. Her car spun out several times before reaching the salted and scraped main highway and, after an agonizing, white-knuckled, two hour trip, Becky and the girls finally arrived at the Manhattan House of Detention.

The aloof, heavy-set, and hostile looking corrections officer at the reception desk in the main foyer of the jail checked their purses for contraband and patted them down before they were allowed to enter the facility. She ordered them to leave their coats and purses in a locker, and coldly told Becky that she and the girls would have to wait in the visitors' area for about an hour while the inmates were having their lunch before they would be allowed to see Inmate McDonald.

When Becky heard Wilson referred to as an *inmate*, she broke out in sobbing tears and her daughters quickly followed suit. The five of them waited for over an hour, huddled together on the cold, hard benches of the waiting area in silence with teary faces until the receptionist finally told them they could see Wilson.

They were led to a large room with a glass divider and a telephone located on each side of the glass. A few minutes later, an unshaven, handcuffed, and red-eyed Wilson, who looked extremely tired and a good twenty years older than his age, was led in by a corrections officer and seated in a chair on the other side of the glass.

Although he tried to project a confident smile and not appear upset, tears began streaming down Wilson's face as he awkwardly picked up the telephone with both of his still handcuffed hands. He spoke with Becky and each of the girls, tried to make light of his situation, and confidently assured them that the authorities had simply made a large mistake that would soon be corrected, and he would be home as soon as possible, probably in just a few days.

With trembling voices, Becky and each of his daughters tried to make conversation with Wilson and express their love between choking sobs. When they were told their visiting time was up, they said their goodbyes, lovingly touched the glass divider with their hands, which Wilson touched back from the other side, and left for the long drive home with sad and teary faces.

*   *   *

On the second day after Christmas, the lavishly furnished large boardroom of Barnett, Breckenridge, and Company, Incorporated began to fill as the fourteen board members slowly filed in and took their seats at the long conference table. The Board Chairman, J. Preston "Press" Noffsinger, then called the meeting to order.

"Good morning, ladies and gentlemen. I want to thank you good folks for taking the time during the holidays to participate in this important meeting, as we must make some major decisions about an excellent investment opportunity for us and our clients that must be evaluated and acted on in just a few days.

As you are probably aware, due to some unfortunate circumstances, our General Counsel, Mr. Wilson McDonald, cannot be here with us today to describe this important investment opportunity in detail for you as we had originally planned, but this situation requires our expeditious attention and decision so we will have to move on without his input. Please remember him and his family in your thoughts and prayers as they face a difficult personal situation.

In Mr. McDonald's absence, Chester Franklin, who has served as one of Mr. McDonald's assistants and is familiar with our agenda, will make the presentation. Mr. Franklin."

A smiling and cheerful Chester sprung from his chair and said, "Good morning, ladies and gentlemen, and a merry Christmas and happy new year to you all. I'm sorry that my friend and colleague, Mr. Wilson McDonald, is unable to be with you today, but I hope you will be satisfied with the presentation that I will give you on this issue and on which I have actually been a key counsel and staff researcher for the past several months.

As you all are probably aware, the reason why Mr. McDonald can't be with us today is because he is presently incarcerated in the New York City's House of Detention, where he is facing a charge of murder in the first degree of one of our employees who had been his administrative assistant."

At this remark, the Chairman sternly interrupted and admonished Chester. "That comment was not necessary, Mr. Franklin. We are all well aware of Mr. McDonald's unfortunate circumstances and wish him and his and Miss Walker's families well. Now please continue on with the presentation and limit your remarks to the business issues on the meeting agenda."

Chester had stayed up nearly all of the two nights before, carefully rehearsing the presentation Wilson had prepared over and over until he had it nearly committed to memory. Using the exact words Wilson had written in his draft script, Chester very articulately described a large European investment opportunity that he believed Barnett, Breckenridge, and Company should consider underwriting and taking a position in, the initial public offering of the shares of the German automobile manufacturer, Goetz Auto, GB.

"I have carefully gathered and studied a substantial amount of information about their manufacturing facilities in Frankfurt, Germany and was deeply impressed with the management team they have in place and the high quality of their products. I am of the strong opinion that Goetz will soon become a key challenger to Mercedes-Benz, which has dominated the luxury automobile sector for many years . . . far too many years . . . and the market is presently wide open and ready for a new leader to step in and replace them.

If we should elect to take a substantial equity position in the company, which I will later describe for you in detail and strongly recommend that you give your approval to, one of our officers will also be provided a seat on their board of directors so that you and our investors will be kept up to date on the status of their operations. I assume that, in the probable continued absence of Mr. McDonald, I will be the logical person to assume that responsibility for the firm."

The Chairman again interrupted and sternly said, "Chester, the decision as to who will occupy the seat on their board if we consummate the transaction with Goetz will be discussed and decided on by this Board at a later time. Now please do not allude to Mr. McDonald's unfortunate situation again and keep your presentation focused on the details of the proposed underwriting and acquisition."

Chester grinned nervously as he powered up the laptop for the Power Point presentation which Wilson had previously prepared. He read through the prospective company's organization, strategic plan, and pro-forma financial projections as the information was displayed on a large screen on the far wall. At the end of the presentation, the Chairman invited the board members to raise their questions.

Following a lengthy discussion, the Board of Directors gave its unanimous approval to the proposed investment transaction. When the meeting ended, Chester was beaming with pride as several of the Board members shook his hand and expressed their appreciation for the excellent presentation he had given them.

The truth was that all of the important work had been done earlier by Wilson, the firm's Chief Financial Officer, Les Wandler, and the Executive Vice President for Marketing, Bill Lovell, something which Chester intentionally failed to mention.

The Chairman had earlier directed Chester to call and ask Wandler and Lovell to be at the meeting to make the presentation, but Chester viewed this as a too highly career-enhancing opportunity for him to let it go by and conveniently failed to do so; then lied to his uncle by claiming that he had tried to reach both Wandler and Lovell, but neither had returned his calls.

CHAPTER SIX

Back at the Manhattan House of Detention, Mark Horowitz and Wilson met in a special small conference room that was provided for attorneys and their clients.

"Wilson, I spoke with your assistant, Chester Franklin, and he told me to let you know the meeting of the Board came off quite well and that the Board gave its unanimous approval to the German investment proposal. He also asked me to send you his best wishes."

Once again, in his uncharacteristic way, Wilson, who almost never used expletives or expressed anger, loudly replied, "That's a whole lot of pure bullshit, Mark! About all that the arrogant little bastard really wishes for me is that I'll be sentenced to life in prison in the naive belief that he'll be my replacement if it happens, which is completely ridiculous."

"You really don't think much of that guy, Chester Franklin, do you Wilson?"

"No, I sure don't, Mark. I was pressured to take the dumb son of a bitch on as an assistant by our Chairman and CEO, who is his uncle; otherwise, I wouldn't have hired him to even rake the leaves in my yard or wash my car. I tried to shape the little bastard up and teach him some things, but he was screwed up beyond repair and I should have fired him a long time ago.

I even had him in my home for a couple of days during Christmas of last year, and the stupid, low-living piece of trash used vulgar language in front of my family and even tried to make a sexual move on Becky. He was so pathetic that Becky and I weren't even offended, because he was so ridiculous, and had several laughs about it later. I'm sure he's enjoying the hell out of this opportunity to be seen by the firm's Board as the hero of this crazy disaster."

"I understand how you feel about him, Wilson, because he didn't impress me at all, either. Well, let's forget about him and take a look at the evidence they have against you. I hate to tell you, my friend, but at this point the situation doesn't look very good.

First, one of the most damaging pieces of evidence they have against you is a clear set of your fingerprints found on the bottle of Scotch whiskey that was held in Miss Walker's hand."

"That's insane, and I really can't figure how that could be, Mark. You know full well that I don't drink alcohol at all and never have, and sure as hell would never even think of wasting my money on buying any of the nasty crap for any reason. And I'd bet anything that Miss Walker didn't drink alcohol either."

Wilson paused in thought, and then said, "Wait a minute, Mark! Every Christmas season many of our grateful clients usually send some of us on the staff gifts, many of them being alcohol, like cases of expensive wine or bottles of whiskey.

I do remember there were some bottles in the office that I usually give away to the other staff members who choose to drink, and I might have been handed a wrapped one by a client and unwrapped it or handed one to a staff member, which could account for my fingerprints being on the bottle, but I don't specifically recall doing so.

But even if I were a murderer, which I'm certainly not, I surely wouldn't have been dumb enough to leave my fingerprints on something so obvious, now would I? I've got to search my memory deeper on that one and try to come up with a definite answer, Mark. What's the next thing?"

"Remember the computer e-mail and the greeting cards that were found in Yolanda's desk which I previously told you about? Although there's no proof indicated that you actually opened the e-mails, they were still on your office computer, ostensibly sent to you by Yolanda, and they definitely suggested that a long term love affair had been going on between the two of you. There were also the greeting cards the detectives found locked in her desk, which were very suggestive and risqué, and were signed only with the initials 'WM.'

A handwriting expert might find it difficult to conclusively prove that you actually handed the cards to her because there was no indication that any of your fingerprints were found on the cards or the envelopes. But from that, combined with the other pieces of circumstantial evidence, a jury would still probably consider them pretty damaging against you, nonetheless.

There's also the eyewitness who claimed that he saw a car like yours driving on Wall Street on the early morning and in the area where Yolanda's body was found. Just like the cards in Yolanda's desk, his testimony could be challenged since the description of the vehicle could have applied to several thousand similar automobiles in the area. But, like I said before, when you fit these several pieces of circumstantial evidence all together, they could collectively work against you in the minds of a jury."

Wilson replied, "Wait a second, Mark. On the night that she was supposedly murdered, I definitely remember that I didn't even drive my car in to New York. I took the commuter train both ways, like I do most of the time, and Becky can testify to that. Shouldn't that fact alone be enough to clear me?"

"You would think so and I sure wish it could, Wilson; however, her testimony would probably be taken lightly and perceived by a jury as a good wife just trying to protect her husband."

Wilson shook his head and sighed. "Whew! So you believe I'm really up against some pretty tough odds right now, huh Mark?"

"Yep, I'm afraid you are, my friend. But I'll keep digging to find the weak spots in their case. I've been able to persuade the DA to schedule your first court appearance in a few days, hopefully by next Thursday, and I know you'll be looking at some stiff opposition from him against your being bonded out. At the least, I know he'll be demanding a huge bail bond, probably up in the millions."

"Quite frankly, Mark, I don't give a rodent's derriere how much money it takes to get it done, because I want to get the heck out of this rotten place and back with my dear family as soon as possible. Please call Becky and tell her to go to our bank and get a certified check for however much money is necessary for the bail bond.

My family needs for me to be at home with them no matter what it takes, and I don't belong in this rat hole of a place. Even though criminal law isn't my field, I also need to take an aggressive role in doing whatever I can to help you in preparing our defense in this ridiculous case. By the way, are you sure that you're okay with representing me, Mark?"

"Of course I am, Wilson; you know I wouldn't have it any other way, but I'll probably need for us to hire a co-counsel who's had more practical experience than I in capital murder cases, especially someone to help in overseeing the necessary pre-trial investigation and preparation aspect of it. Do you know of anyone you'd like to recommend for the job?"

"Yeah, I think I have the perfect guy to help us if he can be available. He's a real good friend of mine from a long time ago in my days at Terry Sanford High School back in Fayetteville and when we were in college together at Chapel Hill. Mike Williford and I were the best of buddies from the eighth grade on, played football and basketball together in high school and college, and we've stayed in close touch with each other ever since.

He's an outstandingly brilliant criminal lawyer in Fayetteville who's about as good as they come. He graduated at the top of his class in School, is one of my best and longest-term friends, and a really great all-around human being.

I recall a major capital murder case that occurred in Fayetteville a few years ago where the defendant was sentenced to die and was within a few days of being strapped into the electric chair at the State Prison in Raleigh. Through some brilliant last minute investigative and legal work on his part, Mike was able to prove the man's innocence by finding the real killer and getting his client exonerated . . . and he even got the guy a compensation of nearly half a million bucks after his release!"

"Okay, Wilson, you've convinced me that your pal, Mike, sounds exactly like the kind of lawyer we need to help us with the case. I'll get in touch with him before our first court appearance and bail bond hearing, assuming that the judge will grant our request for him to serve since he's not a member of the New York State Bar, and see if he can be available to help us." Mark then gave Wilson a warm and reassuring handshake and hug and left.

An hour later, Wilson was told that he had another visitor, his pastor, Reverend Ben Gerrardy, who was waiting for him in a small private visitor's room that was provided them by the Detention Center's Chaplain. After a warm hug and handshake, Ben asked Wilson how he was handling things.

"Not really well at all, Ben. This situation is a totally unbelievable nightmare and it's about to kill my morale and especially that of Becky and our girls."

"I understand, my friend, but it's difficult times like these that show what we're really made of, and I know you are made of the very best kind of stuff. I've visited with Becky and the girls at your home several times this past week and they seem to be growing a little bit stronger each day, even though I know they're still badly hurting and will probably continue to hurt until you've been cleared and found innocent of these wrongful charges."

"Ben, please be straight with me. Do you honestly believe that I'm not guilty of the vicious act they've accused me of and my being cleared of it will be the ultimate outcome?"

"Yes I most definitely do, Wilson, and there's been absolutely no question in my mind or in the mind of anyone who knows you about that. I've known you and your family for a long time and know what you're made of, and you're surely not the kind of person who would ever do anything like the horrible thing of which you've been unjustly accused.

You may be pleased to know that the Church Vestry is one hundred percent in your corner and held a special meeting the other night to see what they could do to help you and your family until this crisis passes, as I know it will. You've always done so much for us over our many years together and we want to help out in whatever way we can to show our love and full support for you and your family.

We realize there's little we could provide you and Becky at this juncture but for all of us to offer our daily prayers for you and let you know we are all prepared to stand up for you in court if and when the occasion calls for it. If you or your lawyer can think of anything else we can do to help you and your family, Wilson, you just say the word and I assure you it will be done."

After few more minutes of light conversation, Rev. Gerrardy gave Wilson a copy of Rudyard Kipling's epic poem, "IF." "Read the words carefully and absorb them, my friend, because they describe you well, as you are indeed the 'sixty-second man'." Wilson recalled that this was his father's favorite poem and he had required Wilson to memorize it when he was twelve years old and would have him repeat it many times over the years. Ben and Wilson then knelt together and said a prayer, and that somewhat helped to lift Wilson's sagging morale. Ben then left and Wilson was handcuffed and returned back to his jail cell.

*   *   *

The large Manhattan courtroom was packed with onlookers and news media people as Wilson was led into the courtroom from a side door, unshaven, handcuffed, chained, and attired in an orange prison jump suit with an armed deputy walking in front of, one on either side, and one behind him. His handcuffs and chains were then removed and he was seated at the defense table.

The bailiff then said aloud, "All rise. This Court is now called to order, with the Honorable Judge Henry R. Mattox presiding."

The tall, grey-haired Judge Mattox then entered the courtroom, took his place at the dais, and directed everyone to take their seats. "This Court will now hear the charges and specifications of the murder of Miss Yolanda Lee Walker of Queens, New York, and receive the plea of the accused, Mr. James Wilson McDonald, the third. Are the prosecution and defense prepared to proceed?"

Mark and the District Attorney both stood and nodded, replying together, "We are, Your Honor."

Seated at the defense table were Wilson, Mark Horowitz, as lead counsel, and Mike Williford as co-counsel. Mike had flown in from Fayetteville the night before and told Mark that his role in the case would be *pro bono* based on his long friendship with Wilson, but Wilson insisted that Mike be compensated at his standard rate. Horowitz had previously requested the approval of Judge Mattox for Williford to serve as co-counsel on the case, which the Judge granted.

After a formal, detailed reading of the charges and specifications against Wilson, the Judge asked him how he pleaded.

Wilson rose to his feet, faced the judge, and loudly said in his deep baritone voice, "I am absolutely not guilty of this offense as charged, Your Honor."

Mark then submitted a normal routine motion for a dismissal of the charges based on the unproven and questionable validity of the evidence presented by the prosecution which, as expected, the judge immediately denied. Mark then requested bail for Wilson, which was strongly objected to by the District Attorney on the grounds that Wilson represented an escape risk due to the possible grave outcome of the trial.

After lengthy arguments were presented by Mark and the DA, Judge Mattox finally consented to release Wilson on a two million dollar bail bond, pending the trial. Anticipating this, Horowitz produced a pre-certified check from Wilson's bank that Becky had given him, in which all he had to do was fill in the amount up to five million dollars, and presented it to the Clerk of Court. The judge stated that the trial date would be tentatively set for two months hence.

Accompanied by Mark and Mike, Wilson was led from the courtroom to a small side room to be processed out. Mark handed him a large plastic bag, smiled and said, "Becky sent these clothes for you to wear just in case we got you sprung. She said she didn't think you'd really want to leave the courthouse dressed only in the bathrobe and bedroom slippers you were wearing when they arrested you."

Wilson shook his head and laughed. "I didn't even think of that . . . don't know what I'd do without that wonderful wife of mine! I sure would have looked weird going out on the street dressed only in my bathrobe and slippers, and would probably get another charge tacked on against me for it, like indecent exposure."

When the paperwork was completed and Wilson was dressed in the jacket, slacks, underwear, socks, shoes, and a wool sweater Becky had sent, he and his legal defense team departed from the courthouse. As soon as they reached the front steps of the building, television reporters jammed microphones into their faces, seeking sound bites which would accompany their broadcasts later on the evening news. Mark made the expected denial of the charges against Wilson, who covered his face and avoided making any comment.

Not surprisingly, the Rev. Anton Jefferson, a well-known black rabble-rouser when it came to high profile cases of perceived racial injustice, had gathered a large crowd of demonstrators outside the courthouse. Egged on by the media-savvy firebrand, they hurtled shouts of "Murderer!" at Wilson as they carried signs protesting, "White Man's Justice" and "Another Black Lynching."

That Wilson's trial would be enveloped by a cloud of racism hadn't been anticipated, and would only add fuel to the fire. There was also a small group of hostile-looking and generally ugly women led by Marcia Stone-Dunham, a hard-boiled man-hating feminist, who carried placards with such charges as "Die Cheater!" and "Protect Innocent Women from Murdering Male Pigs."

Wilson now had three battles to fight, that of not only being labeled a murderer but also as a cheating husband and a racist. He realized with dismay that the court of public opinion would make the legal battle he faced that much harder to win with the added cheater and racist chargess.

Several New York City police officers formed a protective phalanx for Wilson as he proceeded down the courthouse steps amidst screaming insults from the crowd, and entered a chauffeur-driven limousine containing his waiting family which Becky had hired to drive them back to their home in Saddle River.

All the way on the ride back to their home, Becky and the girls clung closely to Wilson, showering him with kisses, tears, and emotional words of encouragement.

When they turned onto their street and approached the gate to their home, they were upset to see many large signs posted on the outer wall: "A KILLER LIVES HERE", "FRY THE MURDERING RACIST," "FILTHY WIFE CHEATER," and several other ugly expressions of hate against Wilson which screamed out at them.

The local television station had a mobile broadcast unit parked outside the gate leading to their home, which was taking videos for the evening news as they drove past it. Wilson had an angry impulse to "shoot a bird" and shout something vulgar at the cameras and news reporters; but his higher self and the presence of Becky and his daughters helped him contain his angry impulses.

Once inside their home, Wilson went upstairs and shaved, showered, and changed into more comfortable clothes. Then he, Becky, and their four daughters sat on the rug in the living room around their beautifully decorated

Christmas tree which was lit for the first time since Wilson had been arrested and taken from the home.

Wilson stood before the large and now brightly lighted tree, clapped his hands together, and announced with a big smile, "Okay, my dear family, we're back together now and we're going to stay that way from now on. There will be no more tears today; so let's get busy with the opening of our Christmas presents and have ourselves the real happy Christmas celebration that we've all been waiting for!"

Becky and the children smiled and even laughed a little, and the gift opening began. The girls happily tore off the wrappings of their many neat gifts, including conservative, expensive, and stylish clothes from Talbot's in Boston, neat monogrammed Coach Handbags, and several beautiful pieces of custom made jewelry from Rhudy's Jewelers in Fayetteville.

Wilson then knelt down before Becky and handed her a small gift box, which she happily opened. It was a beautiful ten-carat diamond and platinum tennis bracelet that went well with her engagement and wedding rings that she had seen at Rhudy's Jewelers and liked during one of their recent trips to their hometown of Fayetteville, and she was thrilled with it.

She handed Wilson her and the girls' gift, an expensive engraved, heavily gold plated, large deep-sea fishing reel and rod which she had had handmade by a well known fishing tackle craftsman, along with cute individual greeting cards the girls had made for him. She then leaned over and softly whispered into Wilson's ear, "Your best

Christmas present is yet to come when I get you alone up in our bedroom, my dear Lover Man."

After enjoying a delicious light snack, the girls put on a cute little Christmas play for their parents which they had quickly thrown together for the occasion. The telephone calls kept pouring in, interrupting the girls' little homemade show several times, and they ranged from highly supportive to downright ugly, mostly the latter.

Wilson finally turned off the telephone and said, "The only people I want to hear from today are right here in this living room, and the rest of the world can just wait their turn."

When the girls' cute and entertaining little homemade Christmas show was finished, Becky and Wilson loudly applauded. Becky then said, "As much fun as it's been, my dear young ladies, I think your poor Daddy's tired and worn out from everything he's had to go through for the past few days, and would like to take himself a little nap before we have our dinner."

The girls grinned and winked at each other. Elizabeth said, "Mom and Dad, my sisters and I are going to go outside for a little while and build us a big snowman, so we won't bother you beautiful folks while you have yourselves a nice little nap."

After the girls had bundled up in heavy snow jackets, boots and mittens and gone outdoors to play in the snow, Becky gave Wilson a seductive look. "Are you ready for a special little Christmas gift from me now, honey?"

"You bet I am, babe! I 'kinda think I know what kind of a present you have on your beautiful mind, and I can't wait to open it!"

"You stay here for just a couple of minutes, honey, and I'll tell you when to come up," Becky said as she dashed up the stairs and into the bedroom.

Five minutes later, Becky emerged from their bedroom, and stood at the top of the stairway, attired in the most erotic outfit in the Fredrick's of Hollywood catalogue. Wilson hungrily dashed up the stairs, shedding his clothes along the way in preparation for their wild, happy, and long overdue lovemaking session . . . and it was one of their most fantastic and longest lovemaking experiences ever, lasting for nearly an hour!

The girls had been briefed beforehand to stay outside for an hour and happily complied, knowing their mom and dad were enjoying each other's love, and this gave them extra needed feelings of security.

CHAPTER SEVEN

Inside his small condominium home, located near the Hudson River in Englewood Cliffs, New Jersey, the thirty-six-year-old Assistant General Counsel, Chester Franklin, who was short, skinny, pale, with a badly acne pockmarked-face and thinning black hair, stood at the bar in his living room and poured himself a stiff drink of Crown Royal liquor on the rocks.

Sitting across from him, looking tawdry with tattoos all over her breasts, back, legs, and arms, with metal studs in her eyebrows, lips, navel, and nose, and salaciously attired in split crotch red panties and a nearly transparent black negligee, was Cassandra Lopez, his live-in, twenty-two-year-old girlfriend. They both puffed on marijuana joints as they sipped their Crown Royal on the rocks.

Chester and Cassandra had been living together in Chester's condo for the past six months. Prior to that, she had studied information technology at UCLA, but ran out of money and dropped out in her junior year to become a prostitute. She was arrested and bonded out by her parents, but then ran away from her home in Southern California to avoid facing the embarrassing trial for prostitution, her third, and one which would surely cause her to do at least a year in prison. This caused her parents to lose their Los Angeles home that they had put up as a guarantee for her bail bond.

Cassandra had hitch-hiked from Los Angeles to New York City and met Chester at an East Side cocktail bar on her first night there. She had broken all contact with her family in Los Angeles, and had no friends or relatives in the New York area . . . only Chester, whom she'd just met in the bar, and she immediately moved into his condo with him.

"I'm on my way up the old corporate ladder now, baby," Chester proudly exclaimed with a big grin in his high-pitched and thick rural southern accent. "As soon as that pompous Harvard shithead, Wilson McDonald, gets what he's got coming to him you'll probably be looking at the next General Counsel of one of the most prestigious securities firms in the whole, wide, freaking world . . . whoopee!"

Cassandra asked, "Does that mean I'll be Mrs. General Counsel after you and I get married, honey, and that you're gonna be earning us lots of big bucks for me to spend on cool clothes, jewelry and lots of neat stuff, and we'll go to fancy parties and take lots of fun trips together?"

He thought to himself, *Oh boy! That's the last thing I want to hear,* as he took a big gulp of the whiskey, wondering how he should respond to Cassandra's very uncomfortable question. He knew it would be necessary to make some major changes to upgrade his personal lifestyle standards once he got the soon to come big career bump up to the position of the firm's General Counsel.

Chester also knew that a heavily tattooed young drunken slut with face jewelry, multiple body piercings, dressed like a cheap hooker and whom he rarely took out in public wouldn't fit in as the wife of the General Counsel of one of Wall Street's most prestigious brokerage firms, so he would definitely have to get her out of his life as quickly as possible.

He thought, *Cassandra's a great little piece of tail, but that's all she is to me . . . just some easy poontang and nothing else . . . and I've got to get her the hell out of my life and become history . . . and the sooner she's gone, the better. I sure as hell won't need the cheap little pig around any longer because I'll be chased by all the good looking women I want when I get my payoff with the big money and become the firm's next General Counsel . . . Whoopee!*

"Why don't you answer my question, Chester? Are we going to get married soon like you've been promising me we would? You told me we were gonna be married way back in September and now it's nearly the end of December and nothing's happened. When's it gonna happen, Chester; when, damnit? Answer me!"

"Uh, I don't know; maybe we'll get around to it one of these days, Cassandra."

"What the hell do you mean by you don't know, maybe, or one of these days'? You said we'd definitely be married by last September and now it's already nearly the end of the year and you haven't even mentioned it for almost three months. You know I need to get married and change my name so the court in California won't catch me.

Were you lying to me before just to get into my britches, or what? Damn it all, Chester, you'd better give me some straight answers right now, you son of a bitch, before I waste another frigging minute of my time waiting for you to get off of your dead ass and do what you promised me that we would!"

Becoming more inebriated, Chester angrily replied, "Shut up your cheap, ugly little mouth right now, Cassandra. We'll get married if and when I say so, and I'm not ready to say so yet; so you better just drop it if you know what's good for you!"

She screamed back at him, "Damn you . . . damn you, Chester! You can't talk to me that way! You shut your mouth, you rotten son of a bitch, and I will not drop it! You owe me big time, you bastard. If I hadn't been able to sneak into your boss's office with you, hack into his secretary's computer and load it with lies, and stuff those raunchy cards you bought into her desk drawer like you told me to, none of this good stuff would be happening for you the way it has.

How would you like it if I were to give your uncle a phone call and let him know all about the things you made me do for you? Or, better yet, maybe I should call the New York cops instead, and tell them the truth about everything. That would sure fix your lying ass real good and put you in a world of deep trouble, now wouldn't it?"

Chester was steadily becoming more inebriated and angry. "You'd better knock off that kind of stupid talk, Cassandra! I told you that you're never to mention that incident again or you can forget about you and me ever getting married, and you can get your ugly little tattooed ass the hell out of my life right now."

Enraged over Chester's insulting remark, Cassandra angrily threw her drink into his face, and this further infuriated him!

In a rage, with the drink she'd thrown at him still dripping off of his face, Chester picked up the thick and heavy half-gallon Crown Royal bottle and hit Cassandra squarely in the face with it, splitting her upper lip and knocking out one of her front teeth. She screamed at him through her bloody mouth, spewing blood all around her, and quickly retaliated by kicking him hard in the groin with her spiked heel shoe.

He doubled over, groaned in pain and yelled, "Okay, you little bitch, now you're gonna really get it!" He grabbed her by her long, straight blue dyed hair and began steadily hitting her about her head and face with the heavy Crown Royal bottle until she finally fell to the floor, unconscious.

As Cassandra lay motionless in a large puddle of blood on the living room floor, Chester bent down to feel her pulse and realized that she was dead!

Panic suddenly seized him as he frantically thought what he should do. *Holy shit, the bitch is dead and I've to get her the hell out of here quick before somebody finds out, or my ass is gonna be in big-time trouble!*

Cassandra's blood, a shattered front tooth, and pieces of her blue hair were splattered all over the living room carpet. Chester ran upstairs to the bathroom and removed the shower curtain, then used it to wrap her body up and sealed it shut with duct tape. He then got a bucket of water, a quart bottle of ammonia, a vacuum cleaner and a sponge, and quickly cleaned up the mess as best he could. He'd give the room a more thorough cleanup later, but first things first . . . he had to get her body out of his house as quickly as possible!

Fortunately for Chester, an attached enclosed garage came with his condo. He threw her wrapped, lifeless body over his shoulder, went into the garage, and dropped her into the trunk of his new black Mercedes-Benz automobile.

Now where the hell can I dump her body so it won't be found and connected with me? Oh, man! Chester racked his brain for a few minutes as he visualized himself being executed or being kept behind bars for the rest of his life for her murder if Cassandra's body should be found and traced to him. He looked around the garage for something essential to his plan for the disposal of her body.

He was startled and jumped back when he felt something brush against his leg. He looked down to see his black cat, Lucky, who had come through the still open door to his kitchen to see what was going on and it gave him an idea . . . *Perfect!* He loaded two twenty pound bags of Lucky's kitty litter into the trunk of his car along with Cassandra's skinny wrapped body.

He then drove down a dirt trail near a marshy area along the Hudson River, located about three miles from his home. Seeing no potential witnesses in this isolated area, he quickly went to work. He opened the trunk and lugged Cassandra's wrapped body out and dragged it close to the water's edge, laying it on the mucky soil that was exposed at low tide. Cursing the way the mud had messed up his expensive imported alligator shoes, he undid the duct tape and pulled open the shower curtain. A shudder went through Chester's body as he looked down at the glazed and wide open eyes on the bloody and swollen face of his dead ex-lover, causing vomit to spew from his mouth.

He turned away quickly and returned to the trunk of his car, from which he retrieved the two twenty-pound sealed bags of kitty litter and placed them on top of her body; then tightly re-closed the shower curtain using wrap-around duct tape. He dragged the bundle across the mud and rolled it into the water, and saw bubbles rise as it slowly dropped out of sight and sank into the Hudson River.

With shaking hands and sweating profusely, he drove back home, carefully wiped the mud off of his shoes, hosed the mud off of his automobile, and went inside his condo, where he drank himself into a stupor and then passed out on the couch.

*   *   *

Chester Duval Franklin was born and raised in a small farm community on the outskirts of Florence, South

Carolina. His mother and father were both well-educated and wealthy but their marriage had become very unstable and turbulent, largely due to the aggravation of raising Chester, who gave them nearly constant trouble from the day he was born, and they eventually divorced.

Frustrated with raising him, neither of his parents wanted custody of young Chester, so they sent him to live with his seventy year old maternal grandmother when he was just five years old, because he was a classic textbook case of attention deficit, hyperactive disorder (ADHD) and neither of his parents could handle him. He remained living in his grandmother's home until she died when Chester was nine years old.

Chester had experienced constant difficulty in adjusting to public grammar school from the beginning, spending much time in the principal's office for various anger-driven misbehaviors, his most grievous one being hitting a girl in his class in the head with his lunch box that required stitches. He often defiantly refused to follow his teachers' directions, was frequently disruptive to the class, and would go into a raging fit any time he was criticized or required to do something he didn't want to do.

After his grandmother passed away, Chester's mother sent him to a private boarding school outside of Charleston, South Carolina, where good grades and a clean record were a guaranteed part of the expensive package.

Upon barely graduating from high school, Chester was enrolled in a small community college for a short while, where he majored in General Studies, which was one of the least demanding academic disciplines the school offered. While there, Chester had a few girlfriends; however, none of them ever lasted beyond two dates when he would always become sexually aggressive toward them.

One female student filed a rape charge against Chester; however, a slick and well-connected attorney was hired by his mother to defend him and was able to get him acquitted by dragging the poor girl's reputation through the mud and making it appear as though she had *encouraged* Chester to rape her.

Chester eventually attended an expensive, small, private four-year college, where he made well below average but slightly passing grades and somehow barely managed to steer clear of any major disciplinary infractions. He was a social loner who soon became addicted to alcohol and marijuana. By sharing his booze and weed, he was helped by one of his very few druggy friends who had hacked into the college's data base as part of a major cheating scheme. This resulted in Chester's graduating with undeserved good grades and receiving a bachelor's degree in Political Science.

Although his score on the Law School Aptitude Test (LSAT) nearly set a new record low, through his affluent father pulling a few strings, Chester was then admitted into a third-rate law school in western North Carolina.

After spending six years in a normally four-year program, he finally barely graduated at the very bottom of his class, thanks to a large donation his father made to the college's building fund. At his parents' insistence, he took the Bar exam six times before finally getting a minimal passing score. He had taken so many previous prep courses for it that he nearly had all forms of the exam practically committed to memory.

After finally being admitted to the Bar, he then went to work in a small, shady law firm in Greensboro, NC for a couple of years where he wasn't well-liked or respected by any of his clients or colleagues. Most of his work had been in simple real estate closings, drawing of wills, debt collections, and other less sophisticated and less demanding aspects of the law practice, which he still often managed to screw up.

After struggling through a couple of years of professional ineptness, resulting in several disciplinary warnings from the State Bar Association, and numerous short-term disastrous affairs with female clients, Chester had pretty well burned all of his bridges in Greensboro. He realized that he had to get out of town pretty soon before his frequent episodes of professional incompetence and inappropriate behavior with women could catch up with him.

His uncle, Preston Noffsinger, who was an honors graduate from the Wake Forest University School of Law, and had several years of high level Wall Street management experience, had recently been appointed to a highly prestigious position as Chairman of the Board and Chief Executive Officer of Barnett, Breckenridge and Company in New York City.

After being nearly driven out of Greensboro, Chester went to New York to see his uncle and pleaded with him for a job on his staff. Reluctantly, as a favor to his sister, Chester's mother, and against his better judgment, his uncle was persuaded to provide Chester with a job as an assistant staff attorney in the firm's large legal department, where he would report to Wilson.

Noffsinger embarrassingly shared the details of Chester's background with Wilson who, being the kindhearted guy that he was, promised he would try to help Chester mature and develop some useful legal skills. That would later prove to be a huge mistake, as Chester managed to screw up nearly every task assigned him, some being costly and potentially damaging to his uncle's tenure as the Chairman and CEO.

In addition to being an incompetent lawyer, Chester had an even more serious problem in his dealings with women. The firm had to brush away three potentially embarrassing sexual harassment law suits from some of the female staff members by slipping payoff money under the table to motivate them to leave without filing formal complaints against Chester and the firm. He even tried to make out with Becky while he was once a dinner guest in Wilson's home, and it was so stupid and pathetic that both Wilson and Becky had to laugh about it afterwards.

Despite this, Wilson still continued to try and see the very little good in Chester, and worked hard to help him overcome his many personality and professional deficits. But, instead of appreciating and benefitting from the help Wilson had tried to give him, Chester deeply resented it.

CHAPTER EIGHT

Mike Williford and Mark Horowitz met in Mark's Westwood law office to begin putting together their game plan for Wilson's defense.

Mike said, "From what I understand in reviewing the DA's case file, Mark, the key evidence against Wilson consists of no more than five basic things: his fingerprints on the bottle of Scotch whiskey, the e-mails allegedly from her to him on his office computer, the risqué greeting cards allegedly from him to her, her boyfriend's claim about the anonymous tip that they were having an affair, and the report of the individual who claimed to have seen Wilson's car on the night she was murdered, right?"

"That pretty well sums it all up, Mike. What are your initial thoughts?"

"Well, the first thing I think we need to do is determine how much of the evidence that the DA has to present against Wilson, which we know is pretty thin and shaky, we can discredit with facts; and then we'll start pulling a stronger case together with our own concrete evidence that will prove his innocence beyond any shadow of doubt.

We both know he's completely innocent, but there's a lot of public pressure being generated by the media to hang him, largely based on the racial and wife-cheater stuff and you know how those things can often override the facts."

"What's your impression of the evidence, Mike?"

"Let's begin with the Scotch bottle that was found in Miss Walker's hand, which seems to be about the most damaging piece of direct evidence they have against him. I've known Wilson for almost all of his life and know for a fact that he's never even touched a drop of alcohol. Didn't you tell me that he told you he had received several bottles of expensive booze from his firm's clients as Christmas gifts?"

"Yes, he did, although he couldn't recall what they were or whether or not he had touched any of the bottles."

"Well, I checked out the prosecution's evidence list and found it was a bottle of Johnny Walker Blue Scotch whiskey that was found in Miss Walker's hand. That's pretty damned expensive stuff and it's not sold in every liquor store. If I'm correct, and I think I am, these very expensive bottles even have serial numbers on them. I'll check with the local liquor distributor and see if we can determine from which retailer the bottle came. Then we'll check with the store that sold it and see if we can be lucky enough to find out who bought it from them."

"What's your point, Mike?"

"Well, if it wasn't one of those that were given to Wilson as a gift, we could have a problem, a big one, especially if it had been bought by him, which is completely impossible;

however, if it was bought by a client as a gift, then perhaps someone else in his office might play into the equation, and it could also better explain why Wilson's fingerprints were found on it. It appears to me that someone in his office could have tried to set him up."

"Okay, that makes good sense. What do you think about the computer stuff?"

"I don't know yet, but I have a couple of guys that I often use to help me with the IT tasks in my Fayetteville office; one by the name of Derek Snodgrass, and the other, my close nephew, Glenn Clark; and when these two guys work together they're freaking computer geniuses who can do just about anything connected with computers.

I'm sure that between the two of them, they will be able to establish what time and day the e-mails that were allegedly sent to Wilson were actually sent, an important fact that wasn't stated on the evidence list. If they were sent at a time when we can conclusively prove that neither Wilson nor Miss Walker were in the office, they would have had to been sent by someone else, probably the real murderer, right?"

"Yeah, that makes good sense, too, Mike. Go on."

"Then, there's the so-called eyewitness who claimed to have seen a car like Wilson's that night. How much do we know about this guy, Mark?"

"He's a night cleaning man for a bank building down the street from where Miss Walker's body was found, who claimed that he had just gotten off of work around midnight and was walking towards the subway station when he spotted the car that was probably carrying Miss Walker's body.

He said it looked suspicious to him, driving as slowly as it was and being the only car on the snow-covered road that late at night. He said he saw it turn into the alley way behind a building at 44 Wall Street, which is next door to Wilson's firm's building and where Miss Walker's body was found early the next day. He said the car had been barely moving, but after stopping for a few minutes in the alley, it suddenly sped away towards the West Side Highway, which is how you get to New Jersey where Wilson lives.

When I first heard that, I checked with the New York and New Jersey Departments of Motor Vehicles and found there are nearly three thousand same and similar looking cars registered in the local area. On top of that, Wilson's wife can testify that he went to and from work on the train, and his car didn't leave their home for over twenty-four hours before and after it was estimated that the girl was killed."

"Well, that's fine, Mark, except we both know Becky's testimony that Wilson went to and from work on the train on that day could be viewed by a jury as questionable and possibly made up to protect her husband, or that he could have gone out later that night in his car. What it boils down to are Wilson's fingerprints on the whiskey bottle, which bothers me the most, the computer emails, and the greeting cards found in Yolanda's desk, and I'll dig deeper into those issues.

When my IT geniuses from Fayetteville, Glenn and Derek, get here tomorrow, I'm sure they'll be able to determine exactly what we need to know about the messages that were allegedly sent from Yolanda to Wilson. These two really bright guys will also analyze the wording and writing style and may find them to be inconsistent with other e-mails she had sent to others. I also want them to give Wilson's laptop a good checking out before we turn it over to the investigators. How much time do you think we'll have to prepare for the trial, Mark?"

"Not a hell of a lot, Mike The DA is determined to get this one to trial as soon as he can to keep the flow of publicity continue going hot like it is so he can do a lot of re-election politicking before the news cameras. I'd guess we have no more than two months to get ready, if that long, because I'm sure the DA will fight us on a trial postponement request."

*   *   *

Wilson had requested and was granted permission from the Court to take his family to their Lake Lure home in the mountains of North Carolina and to visit friends in Fayetteville for the remainder of their children's Christmas vacation, and have some time afterwards to prepare for the trial.

The Chairman of the firm's Board, Preston Nofsinger, had previously requested that Wilson stay away from the office until the trial was over in order to minimize the negative publicity for the firm which his presence might produce, and with which Wilson complied with the understanding that he would remain on the firm's payroll until his case was finally adjudicated.

Wilson had also requested permission to visit his aunt and uncle, June and Todd Lecka, and his other family members and friends in Cumberland County, which was approved on the condition that he must check in and register with local law enforcement offices with each change of his location.

His Uncle Todd was Wilson's deceased mother's brother and a well-known and successful businessman and evangelist, and his Aunt June had been one of his mother's best golf buddies at the Highland Country Club.

He also wanted to visit his father's closest friend and former surgical colleague at the hospital, Dr. John DeBoer, and his lovely registered nurse wife, Diane; his parents' close friends, Marty Sternlicht, who had efficiently handled the settlement of a large part of Wilson's father's estate's life insurance for them, with his lovely wife, Anne, who was another of his mother's golf buddies, and his mother's old friends from college, Eleanor Manning and Mary Morgan, along with several other people from his home town who had called Wilson to offer their encouragement and support to him and his family.

The DeBoer's had extended an invitation for Wilson and his family to stay at their beautiful Oak Island beach home for a few days, and the Sternlicht's offered them the use of their large yacht that they had purchased from Wilson when he moved to New Jersey and kept docked in a marina at Wrightsville Beach.

Wilson, Becky, and the girls piled into Becky's new Chrysler Town and Country van since Wilson's larger and more luxurious and comfortable Mercedes-Benz had been taken into police custody for intensive laboratory tests and was not available to them, and headed south early in the morning.

As they drove south on Interstate 95, they sang Christmas carols, played games, watched videos, and happily chatted about nearly everything but Wilson's legal crisis. They had all committed to each other that they wouldn't mention anything about the forthcoming legal problem during their trip, least it interfere with their fun holiday vacation time in North Carolina.

Before leaving New Jersey, Wilson called his old friends, Drs. Bob and Ann Crummie, husband and wife psychiatrists from the nearby town of Rutherfordton, whose large mountain house on Lake Lure was located next to theirs, and asked if they would arrange for someone to prepare the McDonald's house for their occupancy.

When they arrived at the lake, they were pleased to not only find the mountain house in a squeaky clean condition, a decorated Christmas tree had been set up, a log fire was burning in the large stone fireplace, and the Crummie's had prepared a delicious hot roast beef dinner for them. Wilson and Becky were pleased and determined that this was going to be their finest ever Christmas vacation!

They planned to go skiing, play in the snow, take rides on the lake in the Crummie's pontoon boat, and have a grand time away from all the agony and pain they had left behind them in New Jersey. Although he tried his best to not let it affect their vacation, the anxiety he felt over the upcoming trial was unsupressable and still remained front and center in Wilson and his family's mind.

*   *   *

The Mount Zion AME Church in Queens was filled to its capacity for the funeral of Yolanda Lee Walker, with many attendees having to stand outside in the freezing cold for the service which was broadcast on loud speakers. Several local politicians were present, including the District Attorney, two City Council members, and the Mayor of New York City, and they all gladly did live TV interviews outside the church before the service, each promising the viewers that justice would be served in this case, and implied that they had identified and charged the guilty person . . . Wilson!

Inside the church, there was a lot of singing, praying, preaching, and eulogizing of Yolanda; while outside the church, the same black community organizers that had been at the court house, again led by Rev. Anton Jefferson, capitalized on the occasion by putting on a demonstration and carrying signs that depicted Wilson as an evil man, murderer, and a racist. The feminist group was also there with their accusative signs. As before, the local news media ate it up and were there en masse to cover the dramatic show.

Yolanda's flower-covered closed casket was slowly rolled into the church by the pallbearers, amid tearful wailing and praying by the large gathering.

Her many relatives, friends, and former classmates gave Yolanda warm and touching eulogies; but her fiancée, Tyrone Morris, gave the most stirring and dramatic one of all. In his eulogy, he described Yolanda to have been somewhere between Mother Theresa's love and Oprah Winfrey's brilliance. He spoke of their plans to be married and have a family together, how smart and morally pure she was, how she loved the Lord and their church, and how hard she had worked for a no-good white man who was not only unappreciative of her professional talents, but had used and then brutally killed her.

He angrily ended his eulogy with, "All of the wonderful plans that Yolanda and I had made to share a great Christian family life together were suddenly destroyed by that rotten and evil white man she worked for, Mr. James Wilson McDonald the third, who not only took away the life of our beloved Yolanda when she wouldn't succumb to his sinful advances, but offended all of us who knew and loved my precious Yolanda with his racist hate." He then concluded his eulogy in a loud voice, "May God Almighty cause James Wilson McDonald the third's rotten soul to burn in Satan's eternal hellfire for what he did to our dear sweet angel, Yolanda!"

Tears of anger and sadness flowed down the faces of most of those present, along with shouts of "amen" when he concluded his eulogy . . . except for Yolanda's parents, because they knew Tyrone only too well and weren't as moved by his eulogy as the others and Tyrone would have liked.

As Tyrone spoke, Mr. and Mrs. Walker recalled the occasion about two years before when Yolanda had caught him smoking a marijuana joint and threatened to tell his parents. He became angry and beat her so badly that she had to go to the emergency room for treatment. They also thought back to the time that he was arrested for selling illegal drugs several years before when he and Yolanda were in high school. Although they mourned the loss of their beloved daughter, they had mixed and uncomfortable feelings about Tyrone's sincerity.

*   *   *

Mark and Mike sat together in Mark's conference room, with its long table heavily cluttered with stacks of documents, to review the status of Wilson's case.

"What did you think about how the television media covered Miss Walker's funeral, Mike?"

"It was sort of like I expected and feared it would be, Mark—a big hate show that was well orchestrated by rabble rousers and loaded with a lot of angry emotion. I was especially struck by her boyfriend, Tyrone's, eulogy. It was a little too thick for my money, and I couldn't help but to feel some suspicions about him.

I personally think he's a sleazebag and I was really pissed off when he played the race card the way he did at the church. And the black city councilman, Robinson, really jumped on that one and was playing it to the hilt with Anton Jefferson before the TV cameras after the funeral service. Those angry feminists with their accusations of marital infidelity didn't help Wilson's image either. That kind of unjust and untrue stuff certainly isn't going to help his cause one damned bit."

"I got the same feeling in listening to Tyrone's eulogy, too, Mike; but he had his ass well covered with proof of his whereabouts for the NYPD from the last time Yolanda was seen alive until after her body was found."

"That may have been the NYPD's conclusion, Mark, but I intend to dig further into that guy, and I'll probably depose him before we go to trial. I'm also interested in knowing a lot more about Wilson's creepy assistant, Chester Franklin, because he also strikes me as a slimy guy with no more real caring about Wilson than Yolanda's boyfriend, and he probably thinks he would stand to benefit nicely with a possible job promotion if Wilson should be convicted. My gut feeling is that there's a connection somewhere there with one or possibly even with both of these strange guys and I'm not going to stop digging until I find out exactly what it is.

Meanwhile, I checked with the distributors of the expensive bottle of Scotch whiskey that was found in Miss Walker's hand and found it was definitely delivered to Wilson's office by one of the firm's clients. Several other officers of the firm also received them. The damned whiskey goes for almost a hundred bucks a bottle, so it must be mighty good stuff to the scotch drinkers!"

"Did you get any information from the DA's office about the technical examination that was done on Wilson's car, Mike?"

"Yep, I sure did. It was thoroughly checked from bumper to bumper, and the only thing they found that could be associated with Miss Walker were a couple of the hairs from her head on the passenger seat, but they could have been there from the time when he once drove her home a couple of months ago when she was ill. This event was corroborated by her mother and nothing incriminating was found inside the car or the trunk."

"Well at least that's good news, Mike. What about the sleazy greeting cards they found in her desk?"

"Nothing definite yet, although the initials were made to look the way Wilson usually initialed things with a printed 'WM', so it would be hard to conclusively prove either way. It still looks like a forgery to me, but I can't prove it; at least not yet, Mark, but I definitely will find a way! I found that the cards were purchased at a sleazy sex toy store near Times Square in Manhattan. That simply wasn't the kind of stupid thing Wilson would ever do. I've known him nearly all of his life, and he's never been the kind of a guy who would do something as morally wrong and dumb as that."

*   *   *

Mark placed a call to Wilson at his Lake Lure vacation home on Wilson's cell phone to give him an update on the status of things. Wilson told him he had seen clips from

Yolanda's funeral that had been shown on CNN, MSNBC, and the local television station, and this had really shocked and angered him.

"That one really got way under my skin, Mark! Not only am I not a racist or a cheater, the record will show that I'm exactly the opposite. I've always actively worked against racism and infidelity in one of my church's outreach programs that are specifically directed against those two sinful behaviors.

In fact, I've gotten supportive phone calls and emails from several of Mike and my old African-American teammates from our football days back in high school and at Chapel Hill, many of my old buddies from the Army, and some of my church people who saw it on TV, and they were all really outraged about the racist and cheating stuff the media implied against me because they all said they knew me to be just the opposite.

A young black fellow whose life I saved in Iraq who is now a college professor in Fayetteville has become a close friend since then called me and insisted that he be allowed to come up to New York for the trial at his own expense to testify and let the court know about my saving his life."

"Please make a list of them and email it to me, Wilson, so we'll be able to call them in to testify for you at the trial if we need to."

"Will do, Mark, and if you get a chance, Becky said she would also appreciate it if you would tell those bra-burning femi-Nazis to mind their own business and to kiss her fanny!"

No further mention of the case against Wilson was made in the McDonald family while they were vacationing in North Carolina. They tried their best to make their vacation as happy and normal as possible by avoiding any mention of it but, inside, all six of them were painfully aware that this could be their last happy time together as family.

On the first night at their mountain home, after the girls had gone to bed, Becky began making the seductive overtures that Wilson knew only too well, and sweetly communicated to him that she was in the mood for a relaxing love making session.

During their foreplay, everything had been going pretty well until it was time for Wilson and Becky to enjoy intercourse . . . and he couldn't rise to the occasion! For the first time in their life together, Wilson was unable to have an erection and this threw him into an angry and depressed state.

After several frustrating and failed attempts to function normally, he finally gave up trying, jumped out of the bed, put his head down, and began to weep. Embarrassed and frustrated, he apologized to Becky, who assured him that he shouldn't worry about it.

"I've read about how that this kind of thing often happens to most men when they're heavily stressed out and mentally preoccupied like you understandably are, so please don't worry yourself about it, honey. There will always be better days ahead for us and everything will work okay with you again when all this crazy stuff is over,

I promise. Besides, although you're the greatest lover in the world, I hope you know that I love you for much more than just that!"

But Wilson didn't handle this first-time ever disappointing event well at all, and was sinking into a deeper state of depression, anger, and embarrassment in spite of Becky's attempts to give him reassurance. He went outside for a long meditative walk along the lake's edge to try and work out his feelings, but returned still carrying the same deep feelings of depression and anxiety inside his troubled mind.

CHAPTER NINE

C hester finally awakened from his alcohol-induced coma at about four a.m., and felt like pure hell. His head was throbbing with pain and he was filled with anxiety over the possibility of something going wrong with the disposal of Cassandra's body flooding his worried mind.

He went downstairs and again washed everything he could and shampooed the carpet on which Cassandra had died until he nearly wore holes in it. He also went back into the garage and washed out his trunk and the river mud from his fancy shoes for a third time.

When he felt he had done all he could to cover his tracks, Chester took a shower, put on an expensive Armani suit and headed for the bus station to catch the commuter bus into New York City. He definitely wasn't about to take his black Mercedes outside of his garage for a good while, and planned to keep it locked in his garage for the time being until the heat was off.

When Chester arrived at his office, he found Mike Williford waiting for him in the firm's main lobby. At six-six, Mike stood towering over the small and frail Chester, and introduced himself. "Mr. Franklin, I'm Mike Williford, an attorney from North Carolina, and I apologize for coming to see you without an appointment, but it's very urgent that I have a few words alone with you.

I'll be working with attorney Mark Horowitz from New Jersey on behalf of your and my friend, Wilson McDonald, and I would sure appreciate it if you would take just a few minutes to speak with me. I know you're a busy man, so I'll try to be as brief as possible."

Chester reluctantly agreed to talk with him. "What is it that you want to know from me, Mr. Williford?"

"Just a few things, sir . . . Would you tell me about how long you've known Mr. McDonald?"

Chester nervously replied, "Around two years, I suppose; ever since I was recruited by my uncle, who's the Chief Executive Officer and Chairman, asked me to join the firm."

Chester was clearly uncomfortable in speaking with Mike as he feared that he might slip up and say something to put himself on the spot. In fact, conversing with other lawyers about anything serious had always made him uncomfortable because he knew he was intellectually and professionally inferior to them.

Mike asked, "Mr. Franklin, how well did you know Miss Yolanda Walker?"

"I didn't know her well at all and I only saw her a few times when I would go to Mr. McDonald's, office; the one that they say who was her killer."

Mike ignored Chester's comment about Wilson and asked, "Did you personally spend very much time in Mr. McDonald's office?"

"Not really. I went there only when he called me in and that wasn't very often. I think he resented me because of my uncle, who's his boss and asked me take the job here because he needed me to keep an eye on things for him and help him run the firm."

"Did you ever have occasion to go into Mr. McDonald's office while he was not there?"

That question made Chester even more nervous, and it clearly showed.

"I had to go in there briefly to get his notes on the information for the Board meeting a couple of weeks ago, shortly after he was arrested for murdering his secretary. I don't see what that has to do with anything, so why are you asking me a question like that? What's your point?"

Mike ignored his question and continued. "To your knowledge, would anyone besides Miss Walker and Mr. McDonald have had access to their computers, like their user IDs and passwords?"

"No, I wouldn't know anything about that."

"Did you ever have occasion to use either of their computers, like when you were preparing the presentation for your Board meeting or at any other time?"

Chester suddenly stood up from his chair. "I resent the implication of that question, Mr. Williford, and I don't think that's any of your damned business. Now, if you'll excuse me, I have a busy day ahead of me and I must ask you to leave."

"Why won't you answer my question about the computers, Mr. Franklin? How could you get the information from Mr. McDonald's office for your presentation to the Board of Directors if it wasn't from Mr. McDonald's computer? I don't understand why this question is so upsetting to you."

Chester angrily shouted, "You'd better get the hell out of here right now, sir, or I'll have you removed by our building security people! I have much more important things to do now than waste any more of my valuable time in answering your ridiculous questions about things that are none of your business."

That was the kind of response from Chester that Mike expected . . . and actually wanted, because Chester had responded with such strong defensive emotion about an important element of the case, Wilson and Yolanda's computers. After Chester had ordered him to leave the firm's offices, Mike complied, politely excused himself, and headed directly back to Mark's office in Westwood.

When he arrived at Mark's office, Mark asked Mike, "What in the heck did you do with our boy, Chester Franklin, Mike? He called me about a half an hour ago and said he would seek a restraining order against both of us if either of us ever harassed him again like he said you did to him at his office this morning."

"All I did was just asked the little jerk a couple of simple questions, Mark, but when I began focusing on an issue that was an obviously sensitive area to him, Wilson and Yolanda's computers, he went totally bonkers. I'm going to dig deeper into Chester's background and see what we can find out about him. I have a feeling that we're on the right track with him as a possible suspect because he's definitely trying to hide something. And the next person on my hit list is our boy, Tyrone Morris, to see what he will . . . or won't . . . tell us."

"Mike, you're absolutely amazing! If you're half as good a lawyer as you are an investigator, I can understand why Wilson wanted you to help us on the case."

"To me, solid fact gathering is the most important part of the criminal law process, Mark, and I actually find it much more interesting and challenging than engaging in the canned baloney that often goes on in a courtroom.

Well, I guess I'd better be lining up a visit with our boy, Tyrone. I'd like to get as much of the investigative part of the job here wrapped up this week as best I can, because I have several important cases back in Fayetteville that are waiting for me and I've got to get back and handle by tomorrow.

As soon as you have a firm trial date, Mark, let me know and I'll head back up this way and get to work in helping you to put the trial game plan together. Meanwhile, after I visit with our boy, Tyrone, at his home this afternoon, I'll have to catch a late flight back to Fayetteville. Call me on my cell phone any time you need me, Mark, and I'll see you soon."

*　　*　　*

Twenty-three-year old Tyrone Morris lived with his parents in their neat and modest home in Queens, New York, about three miles away from Yolanda Walker's parents' home, and was employed by New York City telephone call center where he made collection calls on delinquent accounts for a major credit card company.

Several years before, he and Yolanda had attended John F. Kennedy High School in Queens together, where Tyrone was a star basketball player and Yolanda the head cheerleader. They had been dating each other on a fairly steady basis since the tenth grade, and it was sometimes a pretty turbulent relationship.

Yolanda had always been an excellent honor roll student, but Tyrone did only well enough in his academic work to barely qualify him for eligibility to play on the school's basketball team. In the eleventh grade he was arrested for dealing in illegal street drugs and thrown out of school. He was then placed on two years of supervised probation by the court for the offense, and this permanently eliminated his hopes of ever obtaining a college athletic scholarship. Embittered, his anger then took control of his personality and he became increasingly irritable towards everyone, especially Yolanda, who tried to be understanding and help him.

Once, while she was attending the community college, Yolanda broke up her relationship with Tyrone when she caught him smoking a marijuana joint. He became enraged over her rejection of him and shoved her, causing her to fall on the pavement and severely fracture and cut her foot. She went to the local hospital emergency room, where several stitches and a cast were needed to treat the wound he had inflicted on her. A restraining order was issued against Tyrone by Yolanda's father; however, out of her still caring for Tyrone, Yolanda later dropped the assault charges against him and they resumed their relationship.

A couple of months later, Tyrone joined Yolanda's church and was successful in convincing her and her family that he was a "changed man" after he stood up in front of the church's congregation, expressing tearful repentance and remorse for his past wrongdoings, and asked to be saved. Wanting to believe that Tyrone was really a changed person, Yolanda and her parents forgave him and, after they resumed their close friendship, she was even seriously considering a possible future marriage to him.

Mike went to Tyrone's home in Queens in the early afternoon. Tyrone's father, a retired New York City subway train engineer, came to the door where Mike identified himself and his purpose in being there, and asked Mr. Morris if he could talk with him and his son for a few minutes.

"What in the world has that young man gotten himself into now? He's not in trouble with the law again, is he?"

"No, not that I'm aware of, sir," Mike replied. "I'm sure you and your family want to see that justice is done in the unfortunate murder of his fiancée, Miss Yolanda Walker, and I'm trying to gather all the facts related to it that I can for the trial. I hope your son will be able to help me out in this effort by answering a few questions."

Mr. Morris replied, "I thought it was the guy on Wall Street that she worked for who murdered her. That's what I've read in the newspaper and been seeing on TV. My son's already talked to the cops for a long time, and said he told them everything, so what more is it that you want to know?"

"That may be so, sir, and I'm not questioning your son's honesty, but I feel that we owe it to Miss Walker, her family, and your son to be absolutely certain we have all of our facts together so her death can be properly avenged."

"Does that mean you don't think it was her boss was the one who killed her?"

"No, sir, it doesn't necessarily mean that at all, because we really don't know for sure who it was that murdered her. I believe that if her boss was the one who did it, then he definitely should be punished. All I want to do is to make absolutely certain that they convict the right person and the murderer gets whatever he or she deserves to get, whoever that person might be."

Mr. Morris expressed his agreement and shouted from the bottom of the stairs, "Tyrone, get yourself down here right now."

A few minutes later, a tall, thin, drowsy, and sleepy-eyed Tyrone came down the stairs, still in his pajama bottoms and wearing a "do-rag" on his head, and asked, "What do you want, Daddy?"

"I want you to talk with this gentleman about Yolanda, son . . . and I want you to tell him the whole truth about you and Yolanda like you did to the cops, because we don't need to have any more trouble about all this."

Tyrone yawned and asked Mike, "What more do you want to know from me, sir? I already told the police everything that I know about me and Yolanda."

"I just need to ask you a few questions, Tyrone. On the day you were to meet Miss Yolanda Walker at the LaGuardia Airport, do you recall about what time it was that you left to go there and where you went from?"

"I left from where I work in the city at about two-forty-five in the afternoon."

His father interrupted. "That's not true, son. You left from here around noon, didn't you? Remember, you didn't go to work that day because you said you weren't feeling good. That's what you told the police wasn't it?"

"Yeah, Daddy, maybe you're right about that. Wait, I remember now. I left here around lunchtime and went by my workplace to pick up my pay check and get it cashed at the bank so I could buy some traveler's checks for us to use on our trip to the Bahamas. Then I got on the subway to go to the LaGuardia Airport and meet up with Yolanda. I'm not exactly sure about all the times, but I'm really sure that's exactly what I did."

Mike asked, "Tyrone, when Yolanda didn't show up at the LaGuardia Airport for your flight when she was supposed to, what did you then do?"

"I tried to reach her on her cell phone several times, but she never did answer any of my calls."

"Did you leave a message for her?"

"Yes sir, like I told you, I left several messages on her voice mail, but she never did call me back."

"Do you remember about what time it was when you left the airport, Tyrone?"

"I don't remember exactly what time it was, maybe a few minutes after seven, a little while after we'd missed our flight to the Bahamas."

"And then what did you do?"

"I figured she was really pissed-off with me about something since she didn't show up for our flight, or even bother to answer or return any of my calls, so I got back on the subway and went to the Joker's Bar and Grill about two blocks from my house and started drinking pretty heavy. I stayed there 'til a little before midnight, just before they closed, and I was getting 'kinda drowsy from all the booze."

"Where did you go after you left Joker's Bar?"

"I just walked around my neighborhood for a while trying to figure out what the hell was going on with Yolanda and why she wouldn't answer or return any of my calls. I tried to call her again several times; but she still didn't answer, so I decided to call her mother and tell her what had happened. She was worried and said she would call the police and report her as missing. After I did all I figured I could do about it, I went on home to get some sleep."

"Was anyone awake in the house when you got home?"

"No sir, my folks had already gone to bed, so I just went straight up to my room and went to bed myself."

"Tyrone, did Yolanda ever say anything to you about her boss trying to be personal with her?"

"I'm glad you asked that because I think the police got my statement about that one a little bit wrong based on what I read about it in the paper. What I meant to say is that I got a call from some guy who didn't identify himself but said he worked in the same place where she did and wanted to help her. He told me that Yolanda and her boss were having a thing and she was afraid to break if off with him. When I asked Yolanda about it, she told me it wasn't true and I believed her, and that's all there was to it."

"Tyrone, you just said you didn't recognize who it was that called you? I recommend you let the police know about that so they can change the statement that you made to them, because I believe they have a little different spin on it."

"I'll do it sir."

"Do you really believe it was her boss, Mr. McDonald, who killed her?"

"I sure did at first, but now I'm beginning to wonder about it. To be honest with you, I really don't know who it was."

Mike thanked Tyrone and his father for their cooperation, shook their hands and left.

* * *

Mark met Mike for a drink at an Applebee's Restaurant before Mike was to leave for the airport and his return flight to Fayetteville, and asked how the visit with Tyrone Morris had gone.

"I can't really say for sure, Mark, but I will definitely recheck his statement that he gave to the New York cops to see if what he told them tracks with what he told me. Even though he's not the holy one that he represented himself to be at Yolanda's funeral, I do believe that he really did care for her and I don't see him as a very strong suspect at this point."

"Then who do you think could have done it?"

"I still don't know for sure, Mark, but the strongest one to come to my mind right now is that creepy guy, Chester Franklin. I've got to dig deeper into his possible role in it."

"What is it that makes you think he might have done it?"

"I can only say that it's just my gut feeling at this point, Mark, based mainly on the nervous way he acted when I spoke with him at his office, and I sense that he did have a motive, that of believing he would get a big promotion out of Wilson being thrown out of his job. But I think we need to formally depose him when I come back and really grill him good on the hot seat."

Mike then left Mark and headed for Newark Airport and his return flight to Fayetteville.

CHAPTER TEN

After spending four days at their Lake Lure mountain house, Wilson and his family made the five-hour drive over to Fayetteville to visit with some of his close friends and relatives. Wilson especially wanted to have some one-to-one time with his Uncle Todd from whom, during his earlier years, Wilson had often sought his counsel on many personal and spiritual matters.

As hard as he tried to dismiss them, nearly constant thoughts about Yolanda's murder and his forthcoming trial were racing through his troubled mind, along with the additional new anxiety over his erectile dysfunction, which were interfering with his ability to completely enjoy the trip as much as he had hoped. He felt that a strong shot of Uncle Todd's spiritual guidance and advice might help to bring some relief to his troubled mind.

When they arrived in Fayetteville, they headed to Uncle Todd and Aunt June's home that was only a few blocks from where Wilson had lived as a boy. On the way there, they passed Wilson's old family home and this caused a few tears to well up in his eyes as he recalled the many happy times he had spent there in his earlier years. He was reliving some of them in his mind and having deep thoughts of his deceased parents as he drove past his boyhood home.

Becky saw the tears forming in the corner of his eye and understood. She gently touched his hand with hers and said, "I know it hurts, honey, so go ahead and let those tears flow out . . . it'll help with the pain." He choked up and the tears then began to softly flow down his cheeks.

Uncle Todd and Aunt June happily greeted Wilson and his family as they pulled into the driveway of their beautifully decorated home on the sixth hole of the Highland Country Club's golf course. Dr. John DeBoer and his lovely wife, Diane, were also there, as were his parents' friends, Marty and Anne Sternlicht, and his mother's old pals from college, Eleanor Manning and Mary Morgan. Everyone shared warm hugs and handshakes; then Aunt June served a great country style dinner of roast pork, sweet potatoes, cornbread, sliced tomatoes, and turnip greens, which everyone enjoyed.

After dinner, the children went up to bed and the adults, with the exception of Wilson and Becky, who drank only iced tea, enjoyed a glass of wine together out on the Lecka's patio, and talked about everything but the issues that were weighing heaviest on Wilson's mind. After everyone had left for the evening and Becky had gone up to bed, Wilson and his Uncle Todd were left alone on the patio in the darkness.

Todd asked him, "How are you young folks handling your legal situation, son, or would you rather we not talk about it right now? I'm sure it's been a really tough thing for you and your family to deal with, huh?"

"You're so right, Uncle Todd. It's been the worst kind of nightmare you can imagine for all of us and it's caused me to even question my relationship with God, something I would have never guessed could happen to me. I suppose I've always been spoiled and led a sort of charmed life before all this happened, but this situation I'm dealing with now seems so unfair and is really hard for me to deal with."

"Have you prayed about it, son, and asked our Heavenly Father for His guidance?"

"Yes sir, I've prayed over it many times, but it's causing me to even question the very existence and so-called love of God. We talk about justice and how He watches over us, and this seems so wrong that He would allow what's happened to poor Yolanda and her family, and it's nearly destroying me and my mine. I just can't understand it, Uncle Todd . . . I've tried, but I just can't."

"I understand how you feel, son, but there's always a reason for everything that happens to us in our earthly life, and when a lot of rain falls on our heads we have to maintain our connection with our Heavenly Father through prayer until the rain clouds leave and it eventually becomes disclosed to us. As bad as it seems to you now, remember that this too shall pass."

With that, Wilson suddenly stood up from his chair and exploded! "Damn it all, Uncle Todd, please don't give me any more of that holy-rolling pray to God crap or a lot of Bible babble like I've been getting from my pastor back at home! And if I hear that stupid statement that this too shall pass one more time I'll explode. To be honest with you, Uncle Todd, I'm beginning to view religion as a bunch of man-made, wishful thinking crap which benefits the church's bullshit hold on our minds. I never thought I'd feel this way, but I damned sure do now.

I hope what I'm saying doesn't offend you, but I'm about ready to give up on this so-called loving God of yours, Uncle Todd. You've always said that He's a good and loving God. Well if that's true and if He really is in control, then why the hell is He throwing all of this crap into my and my family's life that I've done nothing to deserve?"

"Son, you're obviously not in the right frame of mind now to form that important connection between your earthly and spiritual self. Just keep praying and you'll get past this wall of anger that's formed between you and our Lord."

"I'm sorry to be so negative, Uncle Todd. You can believe whatever the heck you wish, and I'll do the same, but I assure you that our beliefs are anything but congruent right now. As far as all that praying baloney goes, I'm not going to waste any more of my breath or mental energy in doing it because it just isn't working for me."

Todd took Wilson's hand in his and gently said, "Please don't burn the bridges between you and our Lord, Wilson. I understand your frustration over the situation, but don't direct it against Him who loves you more than you'll ever know. Like I've said to you many times before, this too shall pass."

Wilson stood up and sarcastically said, "Yeah, I'm sure He does and that this too will pass, but right now I'm so pissed off that I'm not thinking very clearly." He said, "Goodnight, Uncle Todd," and then abruptly walked away to bed.

*   *   *

The following morning, Wilson and Becky went to visit with his parents' friends, Dr. John and Diane DeBoer, and have breakfast at their beautiful home while the girls went clothes shopping at the Cross Creek Shopping Mall with Aunt June, Eleanor Manning, Mary Morgan, and Anne Sternlicht.

John had recently retired from his surgical practice at the Cape Fear Valley Regional Hospital, and Diane still served as the registered nurse training director at the same hospital. John was well on the pathway to becoming a world famous author, having published three best-selling novels, one of which was under serious review by a major movie producer. Wilson had always held John in high esteem and, although John was nearly twenty years older, he viewed him more as a contemporary and personal friend.

After breakfast, John, Diane, Wilson, and Becky sat outside beside the DeBoer's large swimming pool and sipped coffee while John puffed on his pipe. They chatted and laughed about some of the fun times they had enjoyed together in the past; then Diane asked, "How are you two young folks holding up under all the tremendous pressure of the legal stuff that you're having to deal with?"

Wilson sighed and said, "Thanks for the *young* word, Diane, even though I've been feeling older than dirt these days. To answer your question, we're not handling things as well as we'd like and should be, but we know what the truth is and still hold out some hope this crazy nightmare will come to an end for us one day soon. It's not been easy for me and has been especially tough on Becky and the girls."

"And it's been a whole lot tougher on you, too, honey," Becky injected.

"Yep, it sure has in more ways than you can imagine, but I have some mighty good lawyers working for me and we believe they'll soon be able to make this nightmare go away, hopefully maybe even before there's a trial."

John said, "Wilson, you have no idea how proud your dad was of you during your high school and college years, and I know if he could be with us here today and see how well you're holding up under the tremendous pressure you're dealing with, he'd be even more proud of you."

"Thanks, John, I really appreciate your saying that; although to be very honest with you, I know I'm not handling it as well as Dad would if he were in my position. Becky and I are grateful for the many other wonderful things you and Diane have done for me and my family over the years and your caring support now that we especially need it means a lot. Dad used to always tell me that you walked on water and were really a better surgeon than he."

"I don't know about my being a better surgeon than your dad was, Wilson, because he taught me a whole lot of things about surgery that I could have never learned in medical school, but how did your Dad ever discover my secret that I can walk on water? Was that old dude peeking into our swimming pool?" he asked with a chuckle.

They shared a nice, long chat and had laughs, mostly things about the good 'ole days gone by, and John and Diane offered them the use of their beach home on Oak Island for a few days; but Wilson said they had to decline the offer and get back to New Jersey and start preparing for the trial. "I have to admit that I'm beginning to get pretty antsy about it and have got to get off of my dead butt and start working with my lawyers to help make this mess go away. Besides, the kids will have to be going back to school next week."

After finishing their breakfast and sharing goodbye hugs with John and Diane, Wilson and Becky left to pick up the girls.

After a few brief, drop by visits with a few of their other old friends, Wilson, Becky, and the girls loaded up the van, left Fayetteville, and headed up I-95 north for the long journey back to their New Jersey home.

They arrived in Saddle River at four in the morning, very tired, but glad to be back in their home. When they entered the house, they found a mountain of mail beneath the mail slot on the foyer floor, and their phone voice mail was loaded with messages.

The delivered mail contained a few bills, a couple of letters from antsy banks suspending their large credit lines, many anonymous threatening letters to punish Wilson for his racist crime, and two letters that were even supportive and contained unneeded small sums of cash to help with Wilson's legal defense expenses. One such letter from the National Grand Dragon of the Ku Klux Klan with a check for one hundred dollars and offering the Klan's support was immediately ripped up and angrily thrown away. The majority of the telephone messages on their overloaded telephone voice mail consisted of ugly accusations and threats. Welcome home!

After going through the many phone calls and stacks of mail, they sat down and had breakfast together. Afterwards, Wilson placed a call to Mark Horowitz.

"I just wanted to let you know we're back at home now, Mark, and find out from you if there've been any new developments in the case."

"There's been nothing major that you don't already know about, Wilson, although your friend, Mike, sure has done a whole lot to help weaken the power of the evidence the DA intends to use against you at trial. The damned newspapers and television people are continuing to have a field day, though, and have just about beaten it to death, especially the racist and infidelity stuff. How about you and I getting together at my office tomorrow morning after you're rested from your trip, and I'll bring you up to date on all the details?"

"Will do, Mark. I know I've got to get myself more involved in working with you on my case, and I do appreciate you and Mike giving me a chance to chill out with my family first and get my head on a little better."

CHAPTER ELEVEN

Chester was steadily increasing his heavy drinking at home every night. Late one Saturday night, he impulsively called an escort service which was nothing but a cover up for prostitution and advertised in the Yellow Pages, and asked them to send a young prostitute to his home. About an hour later, his doorbell rang. When he opened the door, a young, attractive, and heavily tattooed Hispanic woman who closely resembled Cassandra stood in his doorway with a big grin on her face. He panicked, slammed the door shut in her face, and ran back inside; then continued with his heavy drinking.

At a little after midnight, Chester finally passed out on his living room couch. Later, he was awakened by his cell phone ringing. He answered it and heard a man's deep voice ask, "Is Cassandra there?" He panicked again and immediately terminated the call, then stayed awake half the night trying to figure out who it was that called and how they knew his cell phone number . . . and he wasn't even certain if it was real or imagined in a bad dream. He was becoming progressively more nervous and, with nearly constant nightmares and hallucinations, had hardly gotten a night's sleep since he murdered Cassandra.

In one of his many nightmares, Chester dreamed that he heard the doorbell ring late at night. When he opened the front door, there stood a mud and blood-covered Cassandra, with a wide grin on her bloody and swollen face, and was still wrapped in the shower curtain. He woke up screaming and was afraid to go back to sleep. These nightmares were becoming steady and progressively more horrible, and made him even afraid to go to sleep.

To cope with these terrifying nightmares, Chester began consuming even larger quantities of alcohol and other mind-altering substances he purchased from illegal drug dealers, but this usually resulted in his becoming nearly comatose at night, causing him to frequently oversleep and go into work late.

One morning when he arrived at the office over two hours after he was due, his uncle summoned Chester to his office. When he entered the office, the firm's nurse was waiting with Mr. Nofsinger.

His uncle stood, pointing his finger at Chester, and said, "Listen to me, you sorry little turd. I hired you to work here; *work* and not drag your lazy butt in here all fuzzy-headed whenever you feel like it. Are you taking illegal mind altering drugs or something, Chester? And don't you dare lie to me either because I know damned well that you're doing something . . . something that's wrong."

Chester angrily denied that he was using anything illegal and claimed that he just hadn't been feeling well lately, probably coming down with a case of the flu, but had come in to work anyhow because he knew the firm needed him to be there.

Nofsinger snickered at Chester's statement, then turned to the firm's nurse and said, "Susie, please get a urine specimen from this man and I want it thoroughly checked out right away for anything that's illegal. I'm warning you now, Chester, if you test positive for anything that's illegal, I will definitely throw your sorry ass out of here for good. But if I'm wrong, which I really hope I am but doubt it, I'll apologize to you."

Chester nervously replied, "Uncle Press, before I left home this morning I took some medicine that I bought at the drugstore for a cold, and that might affect the test. Couldn't we wait a day or so and do the test then? I swear to you that I'm not taking anything that's illegal. I sure hope you know me better than that."

"That just it, Chester; I do know you only too well, and I have a strong suspicion that you're up to some no good. Now you go ahead and give Susie a urine sample like I told you to right now, and don't give me any of that cold medicine baloney."

Chester suddenly became highly offended and indignantly said, "You have no legal right to force me to do that, Uncle Press, and I'm certainly not going to humiliate myself by peeing in a bottle in front of a woman. If you want me to be tested for something, then I'll go to a doctor's office, a male doctor, and I'll get it done; but I want you to know how much I deeply resent your insinuation that I'm doing something wrong."

"I don't really give a good shit what you resent, young man, and don't you tell me about your legal rights! Since you're so bashful about showing your little pecker in front of our nurse, I'll give you two hours to go somewhere else in the area that's legitimate and get a urine test, and you'd better bring the hard copy results back to me before the day ends or you can consider yourself fired!"

Chester left his uncle's office in a worried huff, wondering what he was to do to get out of this jam; then an idea struck him. Prior to leaving the building, he pulled aside a young clerk in the company mail room, and asked if he would give him a urine sample in a bottle Chester provided and keep his mouth shut about it. He said he wanted it to use it to play a trick on a friend. In return, Chester said he would pay him twenty dollars for the bottle of urine.

He took the clerk's urine and went to four walk-in clinics in the Wall Street area that could test him and found only one that didn't require a witness to observe him peeing into a bottle. In the rest room of the fourth clinic, Chester closed the door and emptied the contents he had bought from the young clerk into the test container. The urine tested clean as a whistle and Chester was ecstatic. *I'll teach Uncle Press to accuse me of doing drugs. Now he'll have to apologize to me for his mean accusations. Yes!*

*   *   *

Wilson walked into Mark's office where he was met by a somber-faced Mark. "Hey buddy. I just got the call that we've been both dreading and anticipating from the Judge's office. They've scheduled your trial to begin three weeks from now. I tried my best to get him to grant us at least another month to finish preparing our case, but neither the judge nor the prosecutor would give us any more slack. After I got the call, I called your pal, Mike Williford, and he's on his way up here now from North Carolina to help us. Can you go and pick him up at the Newark Airport this afternoon?"

Wilson told Mark he would take care of that and asked if there was anything he could do to help beforehand. "Just pray real hard, old buddy. This is going to be a rocky road for us. I'm sure we're probably going to be hit with the resumption of a stream of negative media barrages tomorrow after the trial date is announced."

Mike arrived on a US Airways flight from Fayetteville, and Wilson met him at the Newark Airport.

"Hey, Wilson, it's great to see you again, old buddy, although I wish it were under more pleasant circumstances. We've got a helluva lot of work to do to get ready for the big ball game and damned little time to do it."

As they rode from the airport, Wilson asked, "What's your take on where we presently stand, Mike?"

"Well, old pal, we're still a long way from being completely ready to be sure. For openers, I want to formally depose

Chester and Tyrone as soon as possible. I think they're both holding back some information we need that could help you, especially from that skinny little creepy assistant of yours, Chester Franklin.

If I were a betting man, I'd bet my last dollar that he's the guy who did it or at least had something to do with it, but I can't prove it . . . yet . . . but you can be sure that I'm going to keep digging real deep until I find out what might be there to help us."

Mike and Wilson arrived at the McDonald home, where they were warmly greeted by Becky and the girls, and Mark was there waiting for them as well. After a world-class dinner which Becky and the girls had prepared for them, the three men sat out on the backyard deck to discuss the situation.

Mark said, "Guys, we've really got to get our butts into high gear if we're going to be ready for the big show in three weeks. I've basically terminated all of my other activities during this period. You're still planning on deposing the two guys, Chester and Tyrone, aren't you Mike?"

Mike replied, "Absolutely. I sure am and the sooner the better! I'll serve them both with subpoenas first thing in the morning. Depending on what comes out of the depositions with Chester and Tyrone, there may have to be some more heavy follow-up investigative work.

You guys will be happy to know that my IT experts in Fayetteville, Glenn Clark and Derek Snodgrass, got together and checked both Wilson's office and laptop computers and there were no messages ever sent by

Wilson to Yolanda on either of them. And here's the best news of all . . . Glenn confirmed that the messages on your office computer, ostensibly from Yolanda, had been sent on the day *after* the medical examiner claims she had been murdered."

"Good gosh, Mike," exclaimed Wilson, "then who do you think might have sent them?"

"My guess is that it was your little friend, Chester, who did, or had someone else do it since he's probably computer illiterate."

*   *   *

On the following morning, Chester was served with a subpoena from Mark for the deposition and he went totally ballistic! After throwing up several times, having a blasting diarrhea attack, and then chugging down twenty milligrams of Valium to calm his rattled nerves, he finally settled down and went to his uncle's office to inform him about receiving the deposition summons, and solicit his guidance on dealing with the matter.

After showing him the subpoena, Chester asked, "Uncle Press, shouldn't we fight this deposition thing from McDonald's lawyers? Suppose they start asking me a lot of questions about our company's highly sensitive matters or something; business things that are supposed to be kept confidential? What can I do if they do that?"

"No, you stupid ninny, there's absolutely no reason why we should fight your being deposed, especially if it could help Wilson's lawyers get to the bottom of the murder of Miss Walker. They won't ask you any business questions, not that you could answer them anyhow, so I want you to get your sorry ass over there to be deposed and, for once in your worthless life, be a man and tell them the whole truth about anything they want to know. You're sure that you don't have anything to hide about this matter, aren't you, Chester?"

"Of course I don't, Uncle Press, but I just don't like being put on the spot like that. That damned North Carolina lawyer, Mike Williford, insulted the hell out of me last week when he came in, unannounced, and started throwing questions at me that were none of his business and had absolutely nothing to do with the case."

"Just go there and answer their questions, damnit, and stop making a big deal out of it, Chester!"

"Yes sir."

Three days later, Chester arrived at Mark's office, accompanied by a lawyer he had hurriedly hired to accompany him to the deposition and protect him.

They were led into a conference room where Mike, Mark, and a court stenographer awaited him. Chester avoided making eye contact with any of them, and kept his head down when being introduced to each of the lawyers.

Mark began the deposition with a few easy warm-up questions to try and relax Chester. Finally, he asked him, "Mr. Franklin, would you please tell me where you were on the night of December the twentieth of this past year?"

Chester shakily replied, "I was asleep at my home in Englewood Cliffs, New Jersey."

"Was there anyone with you who could verify that?"

Without thinking, a nervous Chester replied, "Yes, my girlfriend, Cassandra, was there with me."

"What is your girlfriend's full name and address, Mr. Franklin?"

Realizing that he had slipped by mentioning Cassandra's name and could have placed himself into deep trouble if her body should ever be discovered and identified, Chester suddenly froze up. "I don't think that's anyone's business and has nothing to do with your case." He then asked his lawyer if he had to answer that question, to which his lawyer replied that he wasn't required to answer any questions he didn't want to.

Chester then froze up and angrily responded to nearly every question that followed with vague and inconclusive replies such as, "I don't know, I don't remember, I can't say for sure, etc." The deposition had turned into a complete waste of time; then Chester and his attorney left!

Mark said, "It looks like we completely struck out with your boy, Chester, Mike."

"It was disappointing to me, too, but his attitude and responses reinforce my belief that he is definitely the guy for us to go after . . . unless Tyrone's deposition should prove otherwise, which I seriously doubt that it will.

I have a friend here in New Jersey by the name of Chris McNamara that I served with in the Army at Fort Bragg many years ago. He's a retired FBI agent who's now running his own investigative agency over in Paramus. If there's anything to be found out about Chester, Chris is the guy who can get it done."

"What do you think your friend might be able to dig up for us that'll help us?"

"I don't know for sure right now, Mark, because I'm still going only on my gut feelings; but I strongly sense that little creep, Chester, played some kind of a role in Miss Walker's murder, and I'm not giving up until we find out what it was. I'll call Chris now and see if he can be available to help us out."

*   *   *

Mike and Chris met at Applebee's for lunch. After sharing some "remember when" stories about the times when they were together many years ago in the 82nd Airborne Division back at Fort Bragg, Chris asked, "What can I do to help you, Mike? I know you didn't travel all the way up here from North Carolina just to have lunch with me and bullshit about our fun times together way back in the Stone Age at Fort Bragg."

"You're right on, Chris. I always enjoy shooting the breeze with you, too, but I do have a very important professional reason for us to meet. I'm involved in helping a close friend of mine who's been accused of murdering his secretary in New York.

I know damned well that he's not guilty, but right now we're playing against a pretty well stacked deck of cards the DA has assembled against him. I'm one hundred percent certain that he's innocent and I think I know who had something to do with it, but I need your help in finding out more about this other guy that I suspect than we presently know."

"Are you talking about the case involving that lawyer from Saddle River named McDonald, Mike?"

"Yep, he's the one, Chris. Wilson is an old buddy of mine from back in Fayetteville and he's as fine a guy as you'll ever meet."

"Apparently the media doesn't seem to think too well of him though, Mike. In fact, from what I've been reading and hearing in the news, it sounds like he's a pretty bad apple, being a racist and a cheater."

"It's exactly the opposite, Chris. Wilson is completely innocent of both the charge of murder and the allegations of racism and infidelity, and I'm willing to stake my life on it. If you're willing and able to work with us on investigating this, I'll set up a meeting with you and Wilson; then, after you two meet, I think you'll agree with me."

"Sure, Mike. I'll be glad to meet with him and try to help you guys out as best I can. The only problem I have is that I'm pretty well tied up on a couple of other cases and probably won't be able to get done with them for at least a month or two."

"Oh shit! That won't work because we're going to trial in less than three weeks. What we need we've got to have inside of two weeks or even sooner, if that can be done. If you can't get away yourself, can you recommend another good investigator in the area for us that might help out, Chris?"

"Hmmm, I tell you what I'm gonna do, Mike. Instead of getting someone else to help you, I'll pass the fairly easy cases I'm presently working on to a friend of mine to wrap up so I can work with you guys instead. You seem to be so set on McDonald's innocence, and I hate to see an innocent guy burn for something he didn't do . . . especially someone from good old 'Friendly Fayetteville' or, as we used to call it, 'Fayette-Nam.' Go ahead and set up a meeting with Wilson and me as soon as you can and we'll go from there."

"Wow, Chris . . . you've really made my day! Thanks, pal . . . I promise you won't regret it, and I know Wilson and Mark will be pleased to hear that you'll be helping us too."

CHAPTER TWELVE

Tyrone's deposition was scheduled for six o'clock in the evening so he wouldn't have to lose any work time. He appeared at Mark's office on time and, unlike Chester, did not bring a lawyer with him.

After the preliminaries were over, Mike started asking the key questions.

"Mr. Morris, you reported to the New York Police investigator that you had once received an anonymous telephone call pertaining to your fiancée, Miss Yolanda Walker. Would you tell me what that call was about and approximately when did you receive it?"

"Yes sir. I received it on my cell phone and the caller told me that my girlfriend, Yolanda Walker, was involved in a love affair with her boss, Mr. McDonald, and she wanted to end it but he wouldn't let her go. The caller told me that Mr. McDonald had threatened to fire her if she ended it."

"Do you recall approximately when and what time you received this call, Mr. Morris?"

"Yes sir. I remember the exact day because it was on the day after I had proposed to her. It was on December the fourteenth, and it was right around noon. I was having lunch at the time when the call came in on my cell phone."

"Did you confront Miss Walker and ask her about it?"

"Yeah, I guess I was real mad at her at first, and said some pretty mean things to her about it that I now wish I hadn't said."

"Did you believe the information that this anonymous caller was giving you was true?"

"I didn't want to believe it because I really did love Yolanda very much and wanted her to be my wife, but I didn't know if what he said was true or not at first."

"What was her reaction when you told her about the call?"

"She angrily denied it and said it was completely ridiculous and even offered to set up a meeting with her boss and me to prove it wasn't so. I then believed her, apologized for acting the angry way I did, and it was all over as far as I was concerned."

"Did you ever hear from this anonymous caller again after that?"

"No sir, I did not."

"Could you describe the caller's voice you heard?"

"It sounded like a white man and he had a sort of high-pitched voice with a strong southern accent."

"If you heard the voice again, do you think you might be able to recognize it?"

"I'm pretty sure I would. I have heard it over and over in my mind many times afterward. I even still hear it in my sleep sometimes when I have dreams about Yolanda." Tyrone began to weep and Mike handed him a Kleenex to wipe his eyes.

"Mr. Morris, do you have any idea who could have killed your fiancé?"

"No, not for sure, but Mr. McDonald's the one that they say did it."

"Did Miss Walker ever speak of him to you?"

"Yes sir, she spoke of him often and described him as the kindest and most honest, clean living man she'd ever worked for. I took her word for it; that's why the telephone call upset me the way it did because I didn't want to hear her talking so nice about some other man . . . especially if he was really the one who was trying to mess around with her."

"Did she ever speak to you about a man by the name of Chester Franklin?"

"Yeah, she mentioned him to me once. She told me that he had rubbed up against her breasts in the company elevator one time, claiming it was an accident, and she had complained to Mr. McDonald about it."

"Did she tell you what, if anything, Mr. McDonald did after she told him about it?"

"Yes sir. She said he called the man into his office and chewed his ass out real good and threatened to fire him if he ever tried to do anything like that again."

"Is there anything else you can tell us now that you haven't already told us or the New York Police?"

"No sir, but if I think of anything, I promise I'll give you a call right away."

"Thank you very much for coming in, Mr. Morris. You've been very helpful and I know that your fiancé would appreciate your honesty and cooperation in helping us to resolve this sad matter."

Tyrone then left the office, and Mark and Mike seemed satisfied with the results of the deposition.

"Mark, we've got to get a recording of Chester's voice and see if Tyrone can identify it as the voice of the person who called him. It sure does sound a lot like him."

"That's not going to be easy, Mike, and we know it won't even be admissible for us when we go to trial anyhow."

"That may be true, Mark, but we'll find a way for getting his voice recorded anyhow. Then maybe we can put Tyrone on the stand at the trial and play it to see if he can confirm that it was the voice he heard. I'm sure Chris McNamara will find a way to get his voice on tape and anything else that we need to know about him."

"I understand, Mark, but couldn't that possibly work against us by corroborating the prosecution's argument that Wilson and Yolanda really might have been having a love affair?"

"No, I don't think so; but if Chester hears this, being the nervous ninny that he is, it might provoke him into saying other things that will point the finger of guilt back at him."

"Good point, Mark. Let's give it a shot and see what it might produce."

*   *   *

Wilson was busily going over pieces of paper from his home files on which he had previously placed his initials with a high-powered magnifying glass, comparing them with a copy of the ones that were on copies of the risqué greeting cards found in his office desk. Suddenly it struck him! The "W" on the cards had a small, almost indistinguishable loop at the bottom. He called Mark and shared this discovery with him.

"I can't understand why the so-called handwriting expert didn't pick up on that, Mark. It took me a five-powered magnification to reveal it, but it's clearly there. Do you think that might be helpful for us?"

"They probably didn't notice it because they didn't want to. While what you've found may not be one hundred percent conclusive it might inject a little doubt into the minds of the jurors and weaken its effect on them. Good job, Wilson! Mike, Chris McNamara, and I are having a brainstorm session later on this afternoon at my office, and we'd like to have you sit in on it with us if you're free."

"I sure will. Who is Chris McNamara?"

"He's an old friend of your pal, Mike, who served with him in the Army's Criminal Investigation Department back at Fort Bragg. He later retired after a twenty-year career with the FBI and runs a private investigation agency over in Paramus, just a couple of miles from my office. I'd like for you to meet him because I think he's going to be a big asset in helping us to dig deeper into the person we now strongly suspect killed Yolanda."

"You're talking about Chester Franklin, huh?"

"You've got it buddy. See you here around four o'clock."

*   *   *

Wilson's girls were playing hide-and-go-seek in their large backyard which went into a roughly twenty-acre wooded county park behind their home. Suddenly, Taylor, who had been the one in hiding, let out a loud scream and her sisters came running to her.

Taylor was lying on the ground, crying and covered from head to toe with a red liquid that appeared to be blood that had been dumped all over her.

"What in the world happened to you, Taylor, and what's all that red stuff that's on you?" her little sister, Sarah, asked.

Sobbing, Taylor told Sarah that two men wearing masks had grabbed her from behind while she was hiding behind a clump of bushes; then held her down while they poured a large container of blood all over her. "They called me the whore daughter of a racist, murdering pig."

When the girls came running into their home, crying and screaming, Becky was shocked and called Wilson, who had been working upstairs in his study. When a sobbing Taylor told him what had happened to her, Wilson ran back upstairs to get his pistol . . . then he remembered that it had been confiscated by the Sheriff's Department since he wasn't allowed to possess a firearm. He then ran downstairs into the kitchen, where he grabbed a large butcher knife and dashed out of the house and into the woods.

As he reached the far side of the wooded area, he saw a small white van racing off out of the park. He couldn't get a clear view of the license plate, but made a strong mental note of the vehicle's description. On his way back to the house, he found an empty plastic gallon container that had blood all over it. He carefully picked it up with his handkerchief and carried it back to the house.

He called the Saddle River town police and an officer arrived at the home within ten minutes. He showed the officer the container and had Taylor tell him what happened. The officer sat at the kitchen table and began filling out an incident report form, but didn't appear to be overly concerned about the matter.

In his frustration, Wilson angrily asked "Well, officer, what are you going to do about it? Why haven't you called this in right away so your people could set up a road block and catch the vehicle that I just told you about?"

"Sir, we can't set up road blocks and tie up our human resources in search of a vehicle that you've barely been able to provide us with a vague description of and no description at all of the occupants. Besides, you people have kind of drawn this kind of thing on yourselves with all the publicity, and yet you still continue living here. Wouldn't it make much more sense for you to move your family somewhere far away from here until after this thing you're involved in is all over with?"

This infuriated Wilson and he shouted back at the police officer. "You people aren't worth a damn to us! I don't even know why I wasted the time in calling you. My daughter has been assaulted and all you do is sit there and write a report of it, and tell us we shouldn't live here where we've been for nearly fifteen years. What in the hell is going on here?"

The officer shrugged his shoulders and said, "You may have a copy of this report if you wish."

"So we can wipe our asses with it?" shouted Wilson.

The officer stood, handed Wilson a copy of the report, coldly said, "Good day, sir," and then left.

Taylor, who had been crying earlier, then tried to calm her father's anger. "It's going to be okay, Daddy. Besides, I wasn't actually hurt. It just scared me a lot and messed up my sweatshirt, tennis shoes, and jeans a little bit, and I'm sure it'll all wash out."

Wilson heard Becky's car starting up in the garage and went out to see where she was going. He tapped the door and Becky rolled down the window.

"Where are you going, baby?"

"I've got to go for a drive by myself, honey, because all of this crazy stuff is finally getting to me real bad. Please just give me a little while to be alone and get my head on straight and I'll be okay. I really need it."

Becky drove out of the driveway and headed towards the main shopping area in the nearby town of Paramus.

134

She then pulled into the parking lot of a local shot and beer honky-tonk joint, The Dew Drop Inn Bar and Grill, and went inside.

*   *   *

At 2:30, Wilson told the girls that he had to attend a meeting in Mark's Westwood office, but would probably be back in an hour or two, and that their mother was out for a drive and should be returning home shortly.

Elizabeth said, "That's okay, Daddy. We're big girls now and can take care of ourselves until you all get back home. We'll even fix you and Mom a neat dinner."

"Okay, Sweetheart, that's fine; but please don't go outside of the house until one of us comes back, and be sure you keep all the doors locked. You can call me on my cell phone if you need me. I love you all." He then left for Mark's office.

Wilson pulled into the parking lot of Mark's office and went inside where he was introduced to Chris McNamara by Mike. The three of them explained what Chris's role in the case would be. Wilson welcomed his assistance and offered to write him a retainer check.

"That's not necessary now, Mr. McDonald. I'm not even sure what, if anything worthwhile I'll be able to do for you yet. I'll charge you by the hour and send you a bill afterwards when I'm done. I just hope I'll be able to help you."

CHAPTER THIRTEEN

After meeting with Chris, Mike, and Mark for awhile, Wilson then headed for home. When he arrived there, he discovered that Becky still hadn't returned from her drive. He asked the girls if they had heard anything from their mom. Taylor said she had called about an hour ago to make sure they were okay, but told them she wasn't yet through doing what she had to and would be gone for a little while longer.

"Did Mom tell you where she was or what she was doing?"

"No, Dad, she didn't say, but she sure didn't sound like herself and the telephone number she called us from wasn't from her cell phone."

Wilson went to the cordless telephone, identified the number Becky called from and dialed it. A male voice answered, "Dew Drop Inn Bar and Grill." Wilson hung up and said, "Girls, I'm going out for a few minutes, but I'll be right back as soon as I can."

The Dew Drop Inn Bar and Grill, a basic redneck type of drinking joint, was located in Paramus, only about fifteen minutes away from their home. As Wilson pulled into the gravel parking lot, he saw Becky's Chrysler van and parked beside it, then went inside the bar.

When his eyes adjusted to the dim lighting, he saw Becky sitting alone at the far end of the bar. She had tears running down her face and, for the first time in their lives together; he saw that she had a large glass of wine in front of her that had been half-consumed, with an empty one sitting on the bar beside it.

He sat down on the barstool beside her and asked, "Are you alright, Honey?"

"Doesh it look like I'm alright Wilson?" Becky replied through choking tears with a slurred voice and a far away look.

"No, it sure doesn't. I'm so sorry that you're hurting so badly, honey, but you know that drinking alcohol isn't going to help the situation one bit. How about letting me take you home now?"

In a raised and sobbing voice she said, "I don't want to go home right now, Wilson. Pleashe just leave me by myself and let me deal with my feelingsh in my own way. I need to be alone right now, so pleashe go away from me and give me some space. I'll work it out."

The bartender overheard Becky and asked, "Is this man bothering you, lady?"

Becky replied in a slurring voice, "Yesh he is. Pleashe make him go away and leave me the heck alone."

"Sir, please stop bothering the lady, or I will be forced to ask you to leave."

Wilson was shocked and frozen in disbelief over what was happening . . . almost as badly as he was when he was first arrested for Yolanda's murder.

He pleaded to the bartender, "But sir, this is my wife, and she's never drunk alcohol before. Can't you see that she's getting drunk?"

"I don't care who she is, sir, she obviously wants to drink and be left alone. For the last time, I'm asking you to leave right now or I will have to call the police and have you forcibly removed."

Becky said nothing but just resumed sipping her wine and staring straight ahead with more tears spilling down her sad face.

Wilson went outside to the parking lot and sat in his car, trying to decide what he should do. He decided that he would have to wait there until Becky came out rather than cause a scene inside the bar that could be detrimental to both of them and could be construed as a violation of his bail bond. He called the girls to let them know he and their mom would be delayed a little while before getting home.

After nearly an hour had passed, Becky finally staggered out of the bar and into the parking lot, falling down several times before finally crawling to her van on her knees. Wilson hadn't noticed her arrival until she had opened her van's door and started the engine. He jumped out of his car and tried get her to open her door, but she had already locked it and didn't even acknowledge his presence by looking at him.

"Becky, honey, please open the door!" he shouted as he banged on the window. But she ignored him and put the car into reverse, and nearly knocked him down. Then she threw gravel as she sped out of the parking lot and on to the main road, Route 17, and headed west towards Saddle River.

Wilson jumped back into his car to follow her, but she had a strong head start on him. As he raced, trying to catch up with Becky, his effort was further delayed by two lengthy red lights.

The traffic on Route 17 was suddenly being held up and barely moving. Up ahead, he saw the flashing blue lights of two Bergen County Sheriff's Department cruisers. When he finally reached them, he saw Becky's van lying on its side. He pulled up behind the police cars, stopped, and raced to Becky, who was still trapped inside the van. The ambulance arrived within minutes and the EMT's were able to pry open the door and remove Becky. Although her van had been nearly totaled, she didn't appear to be seriously injured, but she was clearly drunk and was taken by ambulance to the nearby Ridgewood Hospital emergency room for observation.

Wilson called home to let the girls know that he and their mom would be very late and for them to not wait up for them. Elizabeth took the call and was suspicious that there was a serious problem based on the upset tone of Wilson's voice. She was worried about what was going on with her mom and dad, but didn't share her suspicions with her younger sisters, least it upset them as well.

After spending about two hours in the hospital emergency room, Becky was finally released into Wilson's custody, but was charged by the police with driving while impaired.

Their ride back home was completely quiet, with neither saying a word to the other. When they pulled into their garage, Becky, who had then about sobered up, hung her head low and said, "I'm so sorry, honey." Wilson coldly replied, "Yeah, I'm sure you are, and so am I . . . more than I can tell you." With nothing else being said between them, they both went up to their bedroom and wasted no time in going to bed. There would be no "sleeping pills" to be enjoyed by the McDonald's that night!

Both Wilson and Becky tossed and turned all night long; then finally, at 3 a.m., Wilson got out of bed, went into his study, and opened a book to read and help take his mind away from his troubles.

A few moments later, Becky came in and knelt on the floor beside him, took his hand into hers, and tearfully said, "Honey, I'm so sorry that I made such a fool of myself the way I did. It has been paining me so bad to see you hurting as you have ever since the Yolanda incident began and I finally went over the deep end when Taylor was assaulted. Can you ever forgive me for acting so stupidly, honey?"

Wilson got out of his chair and knelt down beside her and, looking her in the eye as he hugged her said, "Of course I forgive you, my precious wife, because you know I adore you, always have and always will, and I need your love to sustain me." Then, with a loving and sympathetic smile said, "Although I forgive you, honey, I'm afraid the State of New Jersey won't forgive you for the DWI, though, and may make you become a pedestrian for awhile." They hugged each other and went back to bed.

*   *   *

Early the next evening, wearing gray coveralls bearing a UTS logo on the front and a tool belt loaded with what appeared to be testing instruments, Chris McNamara pulled up in front of Chester's condominium in a small black van with a magnetic sign on the door identifying it as a *United Technical Systems, Inc.* service truck. He rang Chester's front doorbell.

Chester had just returned home on the commuter bus from New York, and peered through the front door peephole. Relieved that it wasn't the kind of person who would trigger his anxiety, such as a law officer or a woman remotely resembling Cassandra Lopez, he opened the door.

Chris said, "Sir, there's been a major problem reported in your neighborhood's natural gas line, and I'm here to check out the homes in this area to ensure they aren't in danger of an explosion. May I please come inside and conduct a safety check of your natural gas system? It'll only take just a few minutes."

Chester reluctantly allowed Chris to enter his home, who then proceeded to go through the motions of checking out Chester's kitchen stove and gas fireplace with testing instruments. He asked, "Sir, would you please unlock your garage door so that I can check out the gas lines coming into your home?"

Chester knew nothing about such technical things and gave Chris free reign to move about his home to inspect his system while he proceeded back to his bar and begin his normal nightly routine of anesthetizing his troubled brain with alcohol.

Chester was obviously unaware that Chris was searching for anything that related to his personal life, especially that which would pertain to the woman whose first name was Cassandra or to Yolanda Walker, so Chris's presence didn't seem to concern him.

When Chris entered the garage, the first thing he observed was the black Mercedes-Benz sedan. He also noticed a stack of damp rags, a bucket of soapy water, a bottle of ammonia, a vacuum cleaner, and a large can of disinfectant spray sitting in a far corner of the garage.

Then, while checking the upstairs area, he noticed a dirty clothes hamper in a corner of the master bedroom. He lifted the cover and saw a mud-smeared sweatshirt, pants, a pair of muddy socks, and a pair of blood-stained women's crotchless panties. He slipped one of the dirty socks and the bloody panties into his coverall pocket.

He went downstairs and asked Chester if either he or his wife had smelled gas recently and if there had been any trouble with lighting the gas logs in his fireplace. Chester replied that he hadn't noticed anything wrong. Chris then asked, "Could the lady of the home be available to talk with me? Perhaps she might have smelled something."

"She's not here now," Chester nervously replied.

"Will she be returning soon, sir? I'll be glad to wait for her."

"Why are you asking me these questions about her? What in the hell does that have to do with your inspection?" asked a now very drunk and growingly hostile Chester.

"Because it's been my experience, sir, that the lady of the home is generally more likely to notice things like the strange smells that gas leaks often produce than the man who's been away all day."

Unknown to the now drunk Chester, Chris was recording the conversation on a concealed tape recorder.

"Well, Cassandra's not here anymore and she's definitely not ever coming back, so please drop it. Are you finished with your inspection now, Mr. McNamara?"

"My apologies, sir, and thank you . . . yes, I'm finished."

After Chris left the condo, Chester raced back to his bar and chug-a-lugged another large glass of whiskey to help calm his shattered nerves.

*   *   *

The following morning, Chris met with Mark, Mike, and Wilson at Mark's office.

Chris said, "I now understand why you guys feel the way you do about your boy, Chester. He was as nervous as a pregnant nun when I went to his home last night."

Mike asked, "Were you able to find out anything of interest while you were there, Chris?"

"Yeah, I found a few very interesting things, especially that he owns a late model black Mercedes-Benz that was parked in his condo garage, which I know you'll find very relevant. It also appeared that he had recently done some heavy-duty cleaning of the car. There was a vacuum cleaner, bucket of soapy water, a bottle of ammonia, and a can of deodorant aerosol spray on the garage floor beside it.

I also found some muddy clothing in his dirty laundry basket and a pair of women's underpants that had blood on them." Chris handed Mark the underpants and muddy sock that were wrapped in a cellophane bag.

"He was intentionally avoiding saying anything about a woman named Cassandra; except he said that she was no longer there and wasn't ever coming back. I also got some good recordings of his voice that you can have Tyrone check to see if that was the same voice that he heard on his cell phone. I have some other follow-up moves in mind."

"What do you see as follow-up moves, Chris?"

"I have a woman, a very good-looking and young one, Molly Jean Russell, who works with me on special cases like this one and she's built like the proverbial brick outhouse. With your consent, I'm going to have her call on our boy, Chester, right away, pretending to be a door-to-door opinion surveyor. He drinks a lot, got damned near blitzed in the short time I was there, and is more likely to open his mouth to Molly Jean about personal stuff than to me. That gal really knows how to get a man to talk when others can't!"

Wilson asked, "What do you expect her to find out for us, Chris?"

"I want her to find more about that woman he referred to named Cassandra and anything else he'll say to her that'll help us. She'll get him to thinking that he's a cool dude to her and keep him drinking and talking.

I think he's the kind of guy who'll shoot his mouth off in order to impress her, especially once he's good and drunk. She's smart and will know the right buttons to push to get him to open him up. Maybe he'll even disclose something about Yolanda . . . if he really knows anything about her, which wouldn't surprise me at all; in fact, I'd be surprised if he didn't."

Mark asked, "How soon can you get her on it, Chris? We're running really tight on time. Wilson's trial will be starting in just a couple of weeks."

"I'll get her to drop whatever she's doing and go over to his house tomorrow night."

*   *   *

The next night at a little after six, just as it was turning dark, a seductively dressed young red-haired Molly Jean Russell rang Chester's doorbell and he answered it.

"Good evening, sir. My name is Sally Brown, and I'm taking surveys from the residents of this neighborhood. May I please come inside and have a few minutes of your time to ask your opinion on some important consumer issues?" She displayed a picture ID card on a chain around her neck which drew his attention to her impressive and well-presented cleavage.

Chester was nearly drooling at the voluptuous young woman and gladly welcomed her inside.

"May I offer you a drink, m'am?" Chester asked, as he stared hard at Molly Jean's ample cleavage.

"Why yes, thank you kind sir. I've had a pretty rough day getting these damned surveys done, and a nice cold drink would sure hit the spot."

Molly Jean sat somewhat seductively on Chester's couch while he prepared her a drink of his favorite, Crown Royal on the rocks. Chester sat across from her while she asked him questions from the survey form she had brought with her. She positioned herself so that her very attractive legs would further attract Chester's attention. He was staring so hard at her feminine physical attributes that he was almost in a hypnotic trance, drooling even more, and had trouble focusing on and responding to even the simplest of Molly Jean's questions!

After a few minutes of asking questions relating to his opinion on certain products and issues, and getting vague responses from Chester, she asked to use his rest room and took her drink with her. While in the bathroom, she disposed of her drink of Crown Royal into the toilet, flushed it, and replaced it with some whiskey-colored tea from a bottle she took out of her purse.

When she returned, she found Chester pouring himself another stiff drink and he asked if she'd like another. She gulped down her drink of tea and, shaking the empty glass said, "Oh yes; that one was really good and I would love another."

She had earlier activated the small tape recorder she kept in her purse, with a wireless microphone hidden inside her bra. She didn't have to encourage Chester to talk. In fact, the more he drank, the more he talked and was in a trance from staring hard at her mammary glands. Most of it was bragging about the important job he held and the larger one that would be his any day now; then it soon turned towards what she had been expecting from him and open him up even more . . . sex!

Molly Jean asked Chester if he was married.

"No way," said Chester.

"Then do you have a steady girl friend?"

"Yeah, I had one, but I threw her sorry ass out a few days ago. The way she looked, she was gonna cause me too much trouble in my forthcoming promotion to General Counsel of one of the largest international brokerage firms in the world, because she was nowhere near as pretty or classy as you. How about you? Are you married or do you have a steady boyfriend?"

"No, not really; I'm sorry to say that I'm all alone. So tell me a little more about your ex? Like how was she too much trouble for you?"

"She looked like a slutty tramp; had tattoos, body piercings, and ugly shit like that all over her. I'll soon be promoted to General Counsel of a major Wall Street firm and couldn't be seen with a slutty-looking pig like her. I tried to help her shape herself up, but she only just kept getting worse. I need me somebody that's real pretty like you to show off to my friends and colleagues."

Molly Jean leaned way forward, exposing all but the nipples on her breasts, and this stirred Chester's brain with more excitement. He reached out and attempted to touch one of her breasts. She pulled back and said, "No, not yet . . . not until you tell me more about your ex-girlfriend. I have to be sure that she's really out of your life before you and I go any further together. So, where is that no good bitch living now, what's her name, where's she from, and what does she do?"

Chester was now becoming good and drunk, and replied in a slurred voice, "As far as I'm concerned, the bitch could be dead. If she is, she got what she deserved. Her name is Cassandra Lopez and she's from California, but she's not working anywhere, and never did work except as a whore. Now if that answers your questions about her, how about you and me getting it on now, honey?"

"Okay, Baby, but let's have us one more of those good drinks first before we get started in doing what I believe we both want. Why don't you fix us another big one while

I go to the bathroom again and make myself a little more comfortable?"

Chester poured two more heavy Crown Royals and threw one down with a big gulp, then refilled his glass. *Oh man, I'm gonna get me some fine stuff from this good-looking broad tonight!* In his drunken mind, he assumed that Molly Jean was undressing in the bathroom, and decided to remove his clothes before she came out so he would be ready to have sex her. When he dropped his pants down to his ankles, his legs became entangled in them; causing him to stumble and fall on the floor, striking his head against the edge of the bar. Between the large amount of alcohol he had consumed and the blow to his head, Chester was passed out cold and Molly Jean quickly left Chester's condo with some great taped recordings!

Chapter Fourteen

On the following morning, Molly Jean, Mark, Mike, Wilson, and Chris gathered together in Mark's office to go over the very explicit and somewhat incriminating taped recordings that Molly Jean had collected for them.

Wilson exclaimed, "Wow, this is incredible stuff! It sounds to me like the little creep might have snuffed out his girl friend and I'd bet the farm that a more in-depth investigation will produce the details we need to prove that and Yolanda's murder.

It completely amazes me that the stupid jerk still thinks he's going to replace me as the firm's general counsel because this will never happen anyhow, regardless of what happens to me. The only problem is that while it pretty well indicates Chester to be a bad guy who might have murdered another woman, and certainly could have done the same to Yolanda, it really doesn't tell us anything specific about what happened with her or any proof that he did it."

Mike replied, "That's true, Wilson, but if we can get the Bergen County cops interested enough in the case, they might be able to squeeze more out of Chester, hopefully something that will connect him with Yolanda's murder. I don't think there's any doubt by any of us that he's the one who did it, but being able to prove it still seems to be pretty far away. We just don't have any hard evidence that might connect him to it other than the fact that he has a black Mercedes-Benz, and his voice sounds exactly like the one that called Tyrone.

I think we should take what information we have to Lieutenant Marciano tomorrow and see if we can spark his interest in carrying it further. Although the recordings we have won't ever be admissible as evidence against him in a courtroom, it should be enough to get the Bergen County homicide people interested in looking into what Chester has probably done to the other woman.

What started out as a hunch about Chester being a murdering, sex-driven psychopath is becoming validated, and I still believe we'll be able to somehow connect him with the murder of Yolanda."

Mark said, "I agree with you, Mike, but we're running out of time to get anything done before the trial date, so we need to tie down whatever we're able to and real fast."

Mike replied, "We will, by golly . . . don't know how yet but we will somehow get it done!"

Wilson felt very encouraged by the session and headed home with the most optimistic feelings he'd had about the situation in quite a while. When he entered his home, Becky observed the happy and relaxed smile on his face, the first she'd seen on him in a long time and said, "I have a feeling that you have some positive news to share with me, honey, based on the look on your handsome face . . . one of the first smiles I've seen on you for weeks!"

He shared what was happening and she was also encouraged about its potential for breaking open and solving the case. "Any chance you would be enough in the mood for a little 'ole 'sleeping pill' for us to celebrate this good news, honey?"

He was and they did, and it was a wonderful and sorely-needed experience for both of them!

*   *   *

The following morning's front page of *The Bergen Record* had a surprise story:

Woman's Body Found in Hudson River!

The unidentified and badly decomposed body of a woman was found floating in the Hudson River near the George Washington Bridge early yesterday morning. According to Lieutenant Anthony Marciano of the Bergen County Sheriff's Department, the woman's body was wrapped in a plastic shower curtain and whatever had kept it weighted down had probably broken loose, causing the body to surface. He stated that the condition of her skull made it seem that she had been murdered. She appeared to be in her early to mid-twenties, was heavily tattooed, and had several cosmetic metal pieces in her face.

No identification was found on the body and her description does not fit that of any reported missing persons. The body is presently in the Bergen County Medical Examiner's office for a detailed autopsy and attempts to identify her.

Anyone who might be able to assist in the woman's identification is asked to contact Lt. Anthony Marciano of the Homicide Division of the Bergen County Sheriff's Department.

When Chester read the newspaper article, he reacted in his typical histrionic way by locking his office door and began shaking, sobbing, and sweating so badly that he told the secretary he was coming down with the flu so bad again and that he had to leave work and go home.

As soon as he entered his condo, Chester made a beeline for the bar, began chug-a-lugging his Crown Royal, and was totally drunk within an hour. Every time a vehicle drove past his home, he would begin trembling in fear that it was the police coming to arrest him. He finally passed out.

*   *   *

Mark, Mike, and Chris scheduled a meeting with Lieutenant Marciano. They told him the whole story about Chester and provided him with a copy of the tape recording of Chester's implied admission about Cassandra being dead, along with the bloody underpants and the muddy sock which Chris had found in Chester's home.

Marciano took the information to the Bergen County prosecutor's office and obtained permission to launch an investigation of Chester as a possible suspect in the still unidentified woman's death. However, when this information was shared with the New York District Attorney's office, the DA refused to acknowledge any possible connection between this and the murder of Yolanda Walker, and maintained his firm position regarding Wilson as the killer of Yolanda. A conviction of Wilson represented too precious a political jewel for the DA to let go of that easily.

The Wilson McDonald defense team was sorely disappointed to realize that, although this information stood a strong chance of bringing charges of murdering his girlfriend against Chester, it didn't connect sufficiently with Yolanda's death to absolve Wilson of the charges against him as they had hoped it would. Moreover, Wilson's trial was now only a week away, so any information they had dealing with Chester would be very limited and subject to strong objection as being irrelevant by the District Attorney.

After an intense interrogation of Chester by the Bergen County law enforcement staff and his contradictory and confused testimony, along with the indisputable DNA evidence and Cassandra's fingerprints that had been found all over Chester's home, it became unquestionably clear that Chester was the murderer of Cassandra Lopez. Two days later, the Bergen County Grand Jury issued an indictment against him for her murder in the first degree, and he was taken into custody.

After he was grilled at great length by the Bergen County cops, Chester finally threw in the towel and confessed to killing Cassandra, but insisted that it was done only in self-defense. He claimed she had attacked him with a knife and he had to hit her in order to protect himself and get the knife away from her, and her death was completely accidental.

After having admitted to that much, he slammed shut and rendered only a shrug of his shoulders and a silent and smiling smug every time the interrogators would ask questions related to Yolanda Walker's murder. He steadfastly insisted that he knew nothing about her death and refused to take a polygraph. He was sent to the County Hospital's Psychiatric Unit for evaluation and provided with a court-appointed attorney. They psychiatrist diagnosed him as being psychotic and he was committed to the psychiatric ward at the hospital.

Chester's mental condition was not good news for the McDonald defense team, as it would no doubt preclude his being called in as a witness whose testimony, hopefully, might project his guilty involvement to the jury and take some of the heat off of Wilson.

Also, unfortunately, the trial rules would not allow Mark to make reference to the murder charge that had been filed against Chester. Time was rapidly running out, and their hopes of proving Chester's guilt had basically been stalled by his psychiatric condition.

*   *   *

The day they had been dreading for many weeks had finally arrived. Wilson and Becky arose early in the morning, got dressed in their "sincere blue" suits and quietly drove in to Manhattan where they met with Mark and Mike at a small coffee shop located across the street from the Manhattan courthouse at seven a.m., where his trial was to begin in two hours.

As the four of them had breakfast together, Mark explained what to expect that day. "The first day or two will be spent by the prosecution's presenting of their case to the jury, which is already in place and isn't a bad looking one. They're not the smartest sounding people I've seen, but it's a good mixture of age, ethnicity, and gender, which I prefer in a jury's makeup.

I will be making an opening statement which denies any involvement on Wilson's part and try to communicate that a currently ongoing investigation in another state will soon negate the prosecution's theory. The prosecutor will probably vigorously object to my referring to it, and the judge may chew my butt for even mentioning it, but we'll give it our best shot to get it to the jury anyhow."

Mike injected, "You're right, Mark, and I believe we have sufficient counter-arguments for anything they throw at us when our turn comes for an opening statement, and to posture our witnesses for their testimony."

Wilson asked, "What is the status of the investigation in New Jersey with Chester? Have you heard anything new from Lieutenant Marciano?"

Mike replied, "No, and I'm afraid his situation will remain stalled as long as he's in the nuthouse, and will probably remain so until after our trial . . . but I hope we already have enough on our own without Chester's situation to dilute the effect of the weak evidence the prosecutor has."

At 8:45, the four of them walked across the street, pulling the case files in two large rolling suitcases. Rev. Anton Jefferson had already assembled his crowd of rabble-rousers who were parading around the front steps of the courthouse, drawing as much media attention as possible and Marcia Stone-Dunham, the hostile feminist, and her group were there as well.

After going through the security check at the front entrance, Wilson and the lawyers entered the historic old courtroom and took their position at the defense table, and Becky sat in the first row directly behind them. The remainder of the courtroom was quickly filled to capacity by the media and many onlookers.

At exactly nine a.m., the bailiff announced, "All rise."

With everyone in the courtroom standing, Judge Mattox entered, took his seat behind the bench, and directed everyone to take their seats. He asked the prosecution and defense if they were prepared to proceed with the trial, to which both responded in the affirmative. The District Attorney then began his opening statement,

"Ladies and gentlemen of the jury, we will present a great deal of clear and indisputable evidence to you in this trial that will prove beyond any doubt that the defendant, James Wilson McDonald the third, had the means, opportunity, and motive to willfully take the life of an innocent woman with whom he had used to his advantage of being her superior in the company at which she worked by forcing her into an illicit relationship . . . and when she attempted to end it, he beat her unmercifully until she experienced a painful and humiliating death.

Through the testimony of several witnesses and technical experts, you will reach the inescapable conclusion that the defendant, James Wilson McDonald the third, did indeed murder this innocent young woman, Yolanda Lee Walker, and will find him guilty of a heinous crime for which he should suffer with the loss of his freedom for the rest of his life. Thank you."

After the DA sat down, Mark stood before the jury box and said, "Ladies and gentlemen, what the prosecutor just said to you in his opening statement was based on nothing more than pure unfounded speculation and the use of very shallow, circumstantial, and completely unrelated information that hardly even qualifies as evidence. The truth is that my client, James Wilson McDonald the third, was quite obviously set up by another person to make it *appear* that Mr. McDonald had committed the atrocity which the prosecutor just described.

Contrary to what the prosecutor just told you, he has absolutely no proof whatsoever that my client committed this heinous crime . . . and, in fact, he will present a great deal of unproven and circumstantial information in an attempt to make a connection that simply isn't there; but you ladies and gentlemen will be able to see through this sham and know better . . . then do your important duty of finding him not guilty so that whoever did do this horrible thing may be discovered and prosecuted . . . with *facts* and not an unsupported theory.

We will not only prove Mr. McDonald's innocence with *facts,* versus the prosecution's unsubstantiated *theories,* we will make it crystal clear to all of you that Mr. McDonald has never killed anyone but, instead, has always devoted himself towards helping others. Thank you.

CHAPTER FIFTEEN

Stevens then called as his first witness, Dr. Phillip
Abramson, the New York City Chief Medical Examiner.
After being sworn in, he took his seat in the witness
chair.

Stevens asked Dr. Abramson to state his credentials.

"I am a board certified pathologist with a medical
degree from the Princeton University School of Medicine,
and have served as the City's Chief Medical Examiner for
the past two years."

"Were you the professional who conducted the autopsy
on the body of Miss Yolanda Lee Walker on December
21st?"

"Yes I am sir."

"Would you please tell the court the circumstances
surrounding this autopsy?"

"On December the twenty-first, I was called by the
District Attorney's office and advised that the body of a
young woman had been brought in early that morning.
I conducted a preliminary autopsy and gave my initial
impressions as to the cause of death to the District

Attorney's office. On the following day, I completed the autopsy in more depth and detail, and rendered my final report."

"Doctor, what was the essence of the final report that you submitted?"

"That the deceased had died from several intense blows to her head by a blunt object that created several cerebral hemorrhages and a large loss of blood."

"Doctor, I'm going to show you some photographs which I understand you took during the course of your autopsy and ask you to identify, authenticate, and describe them."

Stevens then put the gruesome photographs of Yolanda's body on an overhead projector and this drew sighs and turning away from looking by many people in the courtroom, as Dr. Abramson narrated a description of the gory details in each of the ugly photographs.

Mr. and Mrs. Walker cried aloud when the pictures were projected and had to be escorted out of the courtroom.

"When you saw the deceased's body, was there anything else that you observed?"

"Yes sir, she had a three-quarters empty bottle of whiskey that had been wedged tightly into her right hand, which was difficult to remove due to rigor mortis having set in to her body."

"Thank you very much, Dr. Abramson. Your witness."

Mark asked Dr. Abramson if, in his opinion, the bottle had been in her hand before or after she died.

"I can't say when it might have been placed there."

"Would it be possible that the bottle was placed into her hand after she died?"

"Yes, it could have been."

"Did your autopsy indicate that the missing contents of the bottle had been consumed by the victim?"

"No sir. When I examined her blood and stomach, I found no alcohol, just a little bit in her mouth."

"Could that little bit have been poured into her mouth after she was dead?"

"Yes, it could have been."

"No further questions, but I would like to have the witness available for recall during the defense phase of the trial."

Judge Mattox consented and so advised the witness.

Stevens continued. "I would like to call as our next witness, Mr. Michael J. Esposito."

After being sworn in, the witness sat in the witness chair.

"Would you please state your name and where you work, sir?"

"My name is Mike Esposito and I work at the Manufacturers Hanover Bank on 28 Wall Street in New York."

"What do you do at the bank, and what are your normal working hours?"

"I work as a night janitor and usually work from six p.m. until midnight during the week."

"Would you please tell the court where you were around midnight on December 20th of this year?"

"I had just finished work and was on my way to the IRT Wall Street subway station to go back to my home in Brooklyn."

"Did you observe anything unusual on your way?"

"Yes sir. It was snowing really hard and I seen only one car on the road, and it was moving suspiciously slow . . . seemed to me like they were looking for something."

"And then what did you observe?"

"I seen the car turn into an alley, stop for a few minutes, then race away. The next day I seen in the papers that a girl's body was found near where the car went and called the police to let them know what I saw."

"Would you describe the automobile you saw, Mr. Esposito?"

"Yes sir. It looked like a brand new black Mercedes-Benz and had a New Jersey license tag on it."

"Thank you, sir. Your witness."

Mark asked Esposito if he had seen the driver of the automobile, to which he replied, "No sir, I did not."

"Did you get the license plate number and are you certain that it was a Mercedes-Benz?"

"No sir, I wasn't able to get the number. The only thing I know for sure is that it had a New Jersey tag. And yeah, it sure did look like a Mercedes-Benz to me from where I was standing. Yeah, I'm pretty sure I'm right about that much."

He pointed to the defense table and asked, "Was the car being driven by the defendant over there?"

"Like I said before, I don't have any idea who was driving it. I never seen the driver and couldn't even tell you if it was a man or a woman or anything about him or her."

Mark shook his head, shrugged his shoulders, and said "So, Mr. Esposito, this car that you saw could have been driven by any one of several million people in New York City and you're not even certain about the gender or anything about the driver, huh?

"Yeah, I guess it could've and, no, I don't know nothing about the driver."

Thank you, Mr. Esposito." DA Stevens winced at that response.

The prosecution's next witness was a fingerprint technician from the New York City Police Department. After being sworn in, he was asked if he had occasion to identify fingerprints found on a bottle of Johnny Walker Blue scotch whiskey on the morning of December 21st and what the circumstances were.

"Yes sir. I was contacted by the County Medical Examiner and asked to remove the bottle from the deceased woman's hand in order to check it for fingerprints."

"And what did your checking reveal?"

"I removed four clear fingerprints from the bottle and sent them in to the FBI lab in Washington for identification."

"And what did you find out?"

"The military records of the defendant were provided to me by the FBI which contained fingerprints taken of him while he was in the Army and they were a perfect match with the ones that I found on the whiskey bottle."

"Your witness."

Mark asked, "Were there any fingerprints other than the defendant's found on the bottle, sir?"

"No sir. I didn't find any other prints."

"Isn't it strange that a bottle which must have gone through many hands before being in the victim's had no other fingerprints? Did the defendant manufacture it and could he have been the only person to have ever touched the bottle?"

"I guess so. I mean, I don't know for sure how they got there."

""Do you mean that it was or wasn't strange to find only one set of prints on the bottle?"

"It was 'kinda strange, I guess."

"No further questions," said Mark as he shook his head to project his disbelief at the witness's testimony.

Stevens then announced that his next witness was none other than Chester Franklin!

With that unexpected event, Mark was shocked and stood up and shouted, "I object Your Honor!"

The judge seemed somewhat surprised as well and asked the two attorneys to come forward to the bench for a side bar discussion. He asked Mark on what grounds he objected to this witness.

Mark replied, "This man was not on the prosecution's witness list and we have received no information about him relating to his role in this case from the District Attorney."

Stevens replied, "We didn't know until late last night that he would be released from being in psychiatric seclusion, and I didn't have time to contact the defense counsel to make him aware of it."

Mark thought deeper and figured that this might be an opportunity instead, and said, "Then go ahead, Conrad, but you'll owe me one for this."

Chester was sworn in. The District Attorney asked him what his job was at the time of Miss Walker's death.

"I was an Assistant General Counsel Barnett, Breckenridge and Company, the largest international investment banking company in America."

"And what was your relationship with the defendant, Mr. McDonald, in this case?"

"I reported to him because he was the firm's General Counsel . . . but in name only as far as I'm concerned."

"And why do you say 'in name only,' Mr. Franklin?"

"Because I really did all the stuff that really mattered . . . like putting together one of the biggest deals in the history of our company while he was sitting in jail for murdering his secretary."

"Objection!" shouted Mark.

"Sustained," said Judge Mattox.

"Did you ever have occasion to observe the defendant with Miss Walker outside of the office?"

"Yes, they used to meet for lunch and I'm sure they did other things as well."

Mark again objected and the judge sustained his objection.

"What kind of things are you sure they did, Mr. Franklin?"

"I can't say exactly, but they were a pretty cozy pair."

Mark again shouted, "Objection!"

Judge Mattox asked Mark to what he objected.

"What the witness has said, Your Honor, is vague, opinionated, and not supported by any fact."

"Sustained."

Stevens then asked, "Mr. Franklin, would you please tell the court on specifically what you based your opinion of the defendant's relationship with Miss Walker?"

"I saw them having lunch together at Delmonico's, saw them riding off in the defendant's automobile, and one time when I accidentally bumped into Miss Walker in the company elevator, the defendant acted like I'd committed some kind of sexual assault on her by his overreaction to something simple like my accidentally bumping into her. It sure did seem to me like something very personal was going on between them."

"Thank you, Mr. Franklin. Your witness."

Mark stood and stared sternly into Chester's face. "Mr. Franklin, can you tell this court when and where it was that you claim you saw the defendant and Miss Walker at lunch?"

"Yeah, it was a couple of years ago at Delmonico's Restaurant, and they looked mighty lovey-dovey."

Mark said, "Your Honor, I request that the witness's subjective assessment of the relationship between Miss Walker and my client be stricken from the record and that he be ordered to answer my questions and not offer such unsubstantiated and unqualified opinions."

The judge concurred and directed Chester to limit his responses to the questions, and advised the jury to ignore Chester's statement.

Mark then asked, "When you claim to have seen the defendant and Miss Walker riding together in his automobile, do you know the circumstances and where were they going? Was it social or business?"

"I don't know why but I am definitely sure that I saw them riding together in his car though."

"Isn't it true, Mr. Franklin, that the time you saw the defendant in Delmonico's was only for lunch and it was on her first day of employment?"

"I don't know when it was or why they were there, but I know for sure that I saw them together."

"Isn't it also true that the time you saw Miss Walker riding in Mr. McDonald's automobile, he was driving her to her parents' home because she was ill and he was helping her?"

"I don't know where they were going or why."

"And isn't it also true, Mr. Franklin, that the defendant once scolded you for having intentionally touched Miss Walker's breasts in the elevator?"

"No. That's not true and you can't prove it. I didn't mean to touch her. It was just an innocent accident that he made a lot of."

Mark smiled, shaking his head in obvious disbelief of Chester's statement and asked, "Mr. Franklin isn't it true that you resented Mr. McDonald for the duration of your reporting to him?"

"Yeah, I sure did because I did most of the work and he always got the credit for it."

"What work did you do, Mr. Franklin, for which Mr. McDonald received the credit?"

At that point, Chester froze up and refused to give any further specific responses to Mark's questions. Frustrated, Mark asked Chester his last question, "Mr. Franklin, do you know who murdered Yolanda Walker?" The prosecutor screamed out his objection and Chester suddenly came apart and began simultaneously laughing and sobbing. He would say nothing more and had to be led out of the courtroom by one of the prosecutor's team and the courtroom medic.

Before the prosecution could call its next witness, the judge closed the court, stating that the trial would resume on the next day.

As they left the court house, Wilson and his team witnessed another surge of the demonstration put on by Rev. Anton Jefferson and Marcia Stone-Dunham that was being videotaped by all the local television stations. They pushed past them and into a rented limousine, which brought strong verbal attacks against them for "being rich."

The news media provided a twisted and biased report in the evening's television and newspaper reports of the first day of trial, suggesting that the prosecution had presented a formidable case against Wilson.

Chapter Sixteen

Wilson, Mike, Mark, and Becky stopped for an early dinner and a discussion of the trial situation at a restaurant in Westwood. As was often the case when they were out in the public, they were immediately recognized by the restaurant hostess as the media pariahs they had become. The hostess was clearly nervous over seeing them and escorted them to a table in the rear of the restaurant.

Becky asked, "Well gentlemen, what do you think about our first day at war? Did we win or lose?"

Mark replied, "I'd have to say neither, Becky. Nothing the prosecutor did today, other than having Chester surprise us, and he didn't contribute much to his case with his crazy behavior, and playing up the fingerprints was not unexpected. I knew they'd try to get as much mileage as they could out of the fingerprints, and will probably keep the spotlight on that one element as much as they can since they don't have anything else with any concreteness to it.

When the trial resumes tomorrow, we'll have an opportunity to weaken his case when we take apart each issue they raised and show it for what it really is . . . plain old shallow sophistry and . . . pardon the expression . . . pure bullshit!"

After they reviewed the day's events and prepared for the next day's continuation of the trial, everyone departed for home.

When Becky and Wilson arrived back at home, they found the girls were very upset and crying. When Becky asked what was bothering them, Sarah told her that the television report made it seem like their father had been convicted or was about to be, and the prosecution was seeking a life prison sentence. Despite Wilson's efforts to reassure them to the contrary, the girls had become anxious from watching the news inference that their daddy was going to be found guilty and they would never see him again.

This characterization of the first day of trial was so inaccurate and reflective of the sensationalizing news media, but Wilson had to accept that the liberal media were not his friends and would probably continue to side with those who viewed him as a murdering and philandering racist. The emotional pain it was inflicting on his family still made him mad as hell!

After a lengthy discussion with them, Wilson and Becky finally calmed the girls down, said their evening prayers together, and turned in for the night.

As he and Becky lay in bed, since she realized that their usual "sleeping pill" wasn't in the cards for that night, she wore her "granny gown" instead of her usual erotic bedtime attire, and just snuggled up on Wilson's shoulder where she remained throughout the night. He appreciated this because lovemaking was also the furthest thing from his mind as well.

After finally falling asleep, Wilson had a strange dream that was incredibly surreal. He dreamt that he and his father were alone out in the Atlantic Ocean on the family's fishing boat. His father's presence seemed so realistic in the dream . . . if it really was just a dream and not some kind of prophesy . . . that he even smelled his dad's familiar Old Spice shaving lotion and the salty ocean air. Although he had dreamt about them many times, this one was unlike anything he had experienced since his parents died . . . so incredibly realistic.

He clearly heard his father speak to him as though he was there with him in the bedroom. "Son, I know things are terribly difficult for you right now, but it's important for you to keep in mind that, even though you're filled with understandable fear right now, this too shall pass and things will eventually become even better for you and your family than it was before all this trouble began. Even the worst outcome to your trial will eventually turn around and be okay, even though it may take some time and cause you a lot of unhappiness before you get there. Remember when I used to tell you that everything happens for a reason? Well, you're going to find that reason for all of this and one day you might even look back on it and be glad for everything that's happened to you, good or bad, so please don't be afraid."

In his mind, Wilson replied to his father. "Dad, I *am* scared to death . . . more scared than I've ever been in my entire life. Not just for myself, but especially for my family. What if something should happen that they would lose me and everything we have?"

"Be strong, my son. If you are strong with your faith in our Lord, what you fear most will never happen, and this too shall pass." And then he was gone.

When Wilson awakened, he wasn't initially sure if it was just a strange dream or some kind of extra-sensory paranormal experience. For some strange reason, just being in his father's imagined presence bolstered his confidence in facing the battle before him with a surge of more courage and optimism. When he got out of bed, he leaned over to kiss Becky and said, "I really believe everything's going to be all right for us, honey. Have faith because I now know that this too shall pass and life will get much better for us than it's ever been." She was uplifted with his confident-sounding optimism.

* * *

They met Mark and Mike at the breakfast place across from the court house, appropriately called *The Barrister's Grill*. The small, crowded place was filled with lawyers with their roller cases and clients with their sad and scared faces.

Mike said he wouldn't be surprised if the prosecution rested its case before the day was over. "After all, they really don't have a whole lot more to offer, except for their shallow circumstantial evidence, and we've diluted what little they've already put on the table by better than half . . . unless they pull another surprise on us like they did with Chester. And I'm sure we'll hear more about those damned fingerprints on the bottle with another dog and pony show."

After breakfast, they strolled across the street to the courthouse and, as before, Rev. Anton Jefferson and his rabble rousers, along with the feminist and her group, and the news media people, were gathered there in full force.

All rose as Judge Mattox entered the courtroom. After everyone had taken their seats, the DA resumed his presentation to the jury.

"The prosecution would like to call as its next witness, Mr. David Evans."

Evans was sworn in by the Clerk of Court.

The DA asked, "Mr. Evans, what is your profession?"

"I am a trained and certified fingerprint technician for the Federal Bureau of Investigation."

"Did you have occasion to examine the fingerprints found on a whiskey bottle on December 23rd?"

"Yes sir. I did."

The DA handed Mr. Evans the bottle which had been found in Yolanda Walker's hand and asked if that was the bottle which he had examined.

"Yes sir. That's the bottle."

"And how do you know this, sir?"

"I recognize it because I placed the cellophane on it to preserve the fingerprints and a stamp that's on the bottom of the bottle to identify it."

"And who asked you to examine it?"

"The New York City Police Department fingerprint lab asked me to corroborate their initial findings."

"And what were your findings based on?"

"The Department of the Army assisted me by providing its file of the defendant's military fingerprint records."

"And what did their report to you reveal?"

"That the fingerprints on the bottle were definitely those of the defendant, Mr. James Wilson McDonald, III. If you will note on the overhead screen there are pictures of both sets of prints and they are a perfect match."

"Thank you sir. I have no further questions. Your witness."

Mark asked, "Mr. Evans, were there any fingerprints found on the bottle other than those of Mr. McDonald?"

"No, sir, there were not."

"Don't you also find that a bit strange, sir? Mr. McDonald didn't manufacture the bottle himself, did he? Shouldn't there have been other fingerprints on it, like some of the many people who probably handled the bottle from its manufacture until it was found in Miss Walker's hand?"

"Yeah, I suppose there should have been, but there weren't any others that were identifiable . . . just the defendant's."

Mark shrugged his shoulders, shook his head, and said "Unbelievable!" He then excused the witness.

The DA called as his next witness, New York Police Lieutenant Matthew DeSessa.

After being sworn in and identified, the DA asked DeSessa to describe the events of the night of December the 20th.

"Early that morning around three a.m., I received a call from a New York City taxi driver who stated that he had found a woman's body in the alley behind 44 Wall Street. I dispatched a squad car to the location and found the body of a lady who was later identified by her parents as Miss Yolanda Lee Walker.

We had her body transported to the Medical Examiner's Office where a diagnosis of murder was established by the pathologist.

As a part of our investigation, we checked the victim's workplace and found items in her desk which suggested that an inappropriate relationship had been going on which involved Miss Walker and the defendant."

The DA asked, "And what kind of items did you find, Lieutenant?"

"We found three pornographic type greeting cards."

The DA produced the cards and showed them to DeSessa.

"Were these the cards you found in Miss Walker's desk, Lieutenant?"

DeSessa looked at them and said, "Yes they are."

The DA asked that they be marked and entered as a prosecution exhibits, which the judge allowed and Mark didn't object. The cards were then projected on to a large screen for the jury to see and they were extremely risqué and graphic, bringing mumbling and snickering that was heard throughout the courtroom, causing Judge Mattox to rap his gavel to restore order.

The DA asked DeSessa who he thought might have given them to Miss Walker, and DeSessa replied that the defendant's initials were on them.

"And how do you know the initials were those of the defendant?"

"We assumed they were because they were a W and an M and looked exactly like the initials that he had placed on other documents that were on and inside his desk. We had our handwriting analyst check them and he reported that they were very similar in size and shape, and could have been made by the same person."

"Thank you, Lieutenant DeSessa. Your witness."

Mark asked DeSessa, "Did your handwriting analyst say that the initials on the cards were definitely made by the defendant or just that they could have been?"

"Could have been."

"In other words, Lieutenant, those initials could have been made by anyone, correct?"

"Yes sir, I guess so."

"You guess so? Lieutenant, we're dealing with a man's life here and are using so-called evidence which your investigation produced that 'could have been' to convict him of a murder that he did not commit! I have no further questions of this 'could have been' witness."

The DA's next witness was Tyrone Morris.

After he was sworn in, the DA asked him to identify himself and his relationship to the victim.

"My name is Tyrone Morris and I was Miss Yolanda Walker's proud fiancée.

"Do you know the defendant in this case?"

"No sir, I don't know him personally."

"In what way did you know of him?"

"My fiancée worked for him and I've seen him a couple of times."

"Did your fiancée tell you anything about him? Like was he a good or bad boss?"

"She bragged about him all the time. She said he was the best boss in the world to work for."

"Mr. Morris, did there ever come a time when you found yourself feeling negatively toward Mr. McDonald?"

"Yeah, there sure was."

"Would you describe what it was that made you feel this way?"

"Some guy called me on my cell phone and said some ugly stuff about Mr. McDonald and my fiancée."

"What did he say to you?"

"He said that Yolanda and Mr. McDonald had been having an affair together and he wouldn't break it off."

"Thank you, Mr. Morris. Your witness."

Mark asked, "Mr. Morris, did you have any reason to distrust your fiancée by believing what this person said to you about her and her boss?"

"No, sir, I didn't want to believe it when I first heard it and I don't believe it now."

"Could you describe this mystery voice that you heard on your cell phone?"

"Yes sir, it was from a white man with a high-pitched voice and a strong southern accent."

"And you didn't know who it was that called you?"

"No sir, I didn't."

"You've heard Mr. McDonald's voice before, haven't you?"

"Yes I have and it definitely wasn't him that I heard on my phone."

"And you heard the voice of the last witness, Mr. Franklin, didn't you?"

The DA shouted "Objection!"

Judge Mattox sustained the DA's objection and told the jury to ignore the question.

Mark then excused the witness.

With that, the DA said, "the Prosecution rests."

Judge Mattox then ordered a recess for lunch, with the trial to resume in two hours.

As Wilson, Becky, Mark, and Mike sat at the diner having lunch, Wilson asked, "Well, what are your thoughts now, Mark? Are we winning or losing?"

"At this point, old buddy, I think we're ahead but only by a few points. If our presentation isn't ripped up by the DA, which I don't expect or know how it could be, we should be in pretty good shape for the verdict we want. The jerk tried to keep the jury focused on the fingerprint issue by bringing in not one, but two experts and putting on that stupid dog and pony show. I may recall them and try to further tear their findings to ribbons."

As they quietly ate their lunch, Mike asked Mark "What are your thoughts about putting Wilson on the stand?"

"I'm not real sure right now, Mike, and it's rare to never that I would have a defendant to testify in a case like this, but my gut tells me that it might work for us in this instance. What are your thoughts about it?"

"I agree with you and think it would be a strong and dramatic way to wrap up our presentation. In fact, I think that both Wilson and Becky should testify, with Becky being first. Wilson looks like anything but a cheating racist murder, and Becky's obvious loyalty to and belief in him would help to reinforce the image of the loyal and loving husband he is and we want the jury to see him as."

As they were talking, the television set in the restaurant was turned on to the local news report. Showing a photograph of both Wilson and Yolanda, the announcer said, "At noon today, the prosecution rested its case in the murder trial of James Wilson McDonald, III and the defense will begin its presentation this afternoon.

McDonald is accused of murdering his office assistant, a young African-American woman back in December, and is the target of several local civil rights organizations for racist and philandering behavior. If convicted, he faces the rest of his life in prison. Meanwhile, the District Attorney expressed that he feels the State has more than proven his case against McDonald. We will give you an update later on the six o'clock news."

Hearing this biased and twisted news report cast a gloomy spell on the gathering, and they arose and headed back to the court house.

CHAPTER SEVENTEEN

After Judge Mattox entered the courtroom and those present were seated, Mark stood and said, "Your Honor and ladies and gentlemen of the jury, the defense in this case is prepared to disprove the allegations made by the prosecution and prove beyond any shadow of doubt that the defendant, James Wilson McDonald the third, is innocent of the charges against him. We will now call as our first witness, Dr. Deshawn Jackson."

Jackson was sworn in and seated in the witness chair.

After he was seated, Mark asked Jackson, "What do you do for a living, sir?"

"After I was medically discharged from the Army about fifteen years ago, I earned a doctorate degree in mathematics from North Carolina State University in Raleigh, and currently serve as a professor of mathematics at the Fayetteville State University in Cumberland County, North Carolina."

"Do you know the defendant in this case, Dr. Jackson?"

"Yes, I've known him very well for nearly twenty years."

"Are you aware of the charges that have been made against Mr. McDonald?"

"I am."

"And would you tell this court your impressions of them?"

"The most outrageous lies I've ever heard, especially the media allegations that Mr. McDonald is a racist and a philanderer. If there was ever a white man who cared about his fellow man and his family, regardless of their race, it is Mr. McDonald."

"Please tell the court how you got to know him."

"I first knew him as Lieutenant McDonald and I was a private first class when we served together in the 82d Airborne Division. He risked his life to save mine while we were deployed together in the Army in the Middle East, and it cost him a career in professional football due to the wound he got when he saved me from what would have been a certain death. Since that time, we have stayed in close touch with each other and are the best of friends."

"Do you believe that Mr. McDonald would have an illicit relationship with a woman and kill her?"

"Absolutely not! This good man wouldn't kill a fly, and his morals are so high that having such a relationship with any woman other than his beautiful wife would be totally out of his high character."

"Thank you, Dr. Jackson. Your witness."

The DA rolled his eyes as though what had been said had no significance and said, "I have no questions."

Mark called his next witness, James Curtis.

Curtis appeared in his Am Track conductor's uniform and was sworn in by the clerk of court.

Mark asked Curtis to identify himself and state his occupation.

"My name is James L. Curtis and I serve as a conductor on the Am Track commuter train division which is headquartered in Newark, New Jersey."

"Do you know the defendant in this case? If so, please point to him and state his name."

Curtis replied as he pointed to Wilson, "Mr. McDonald,"

"And approximately how long have you known Mr. McDonald?"

"A pretty good while; I'd say at least five or six years . . . ever since I started working as a conductor on the train that he catches almost every weekday from the Westwood, New Jersey station to Pennsylvania Station in New York and back."

"In what capacity did you get to know him?"

"I served as the conductor of the train and he was a pretty regular passenger on my route."

"Do you recall seeing Mr. McDonald on the early evening train from New York to Westwood on December 20th?"

"Yes, I most certainly do. I remember it well; not only because I've known him for a long time, but also because he gave me nice Christmas gift tip in a Christmas card that day."

"A what sir?"

"A few of my passengers are thoughtful enough each year to give me a Christmas gift of a tip, usually in the form of money, and Mr. McDonald has always been extremely generous to me. That's why he 'kinda stands out in my mind."

"Do you recall how much money he gave you, sir, and in what form?"

"He gave me a check for one hundred dollars in a nice Christmas card."

"And what did you do with the check?"

"I deposited it in my bank account and figured you might want to see some proof of it so I brought the deposit receipt for it here with me today."

Curtis then opened his wallet and handed the receipt to Mark, who asked that it be entered into evidence as defense exhibit #1, to which the DA didn't object.

Mark asked, "Do you recall approximately what time it was when you saw Mr. McDonald on the train on the twentieth of December?"

"Yes, sir, it was about five thirty-two, give or take a minute. The train had just begun its exit out of the Pennsylvania Railroad Station, and it always leaves exactly on time. Mr. McDonald handed me his ticket and the envelope just as the train was departing from the station."

"Thank you, Mr. Curtis. I have no further questions. Your witness."

The DA asked, "When your passengers give you Christmas gifts of money, are the gifts usually in cash or checks?"

Curtis thought for a moment and replied, "It's usually cash."

"Did Mr. McDonald give you a check or cash for a Christmas gift in previous years?"

"I'm pretty sure it was always cash before. I was so honored to have his check since he's so well known that I even thought about saving it instead of cashing it."

"Were there other passengers on the train beside Mr. McDonald?"

"Of course there were. We're always loaded up on that run since it's the start of the go-home traffic each day."

"Did anyone else give you a Christmas gift that day?"

"I think so . . . I'm pretty sure they did."

"You're completely sure that Mr. McDonald did, but only pretty sure that others did?"

"Yeah, I'm pretty sure."

The DA went to the evidence table, picked up the deposit ticket, and handed it to Curtis.

"Mr. Curtis, would you look closely at the deposit ticket you provided us and tell me if it shows any information about Mr. McDonald's check?"

Curtis stared at the ticket and then replied, "It doesn't say. It only says a hundred dollars."

"In other words isn't it true that it could have been anyone's check dated any day, and not necessarily that of Mr. McDonald?"

"Yeah, I guess it could."

"You guess it could . . . ."

The DA threw up his hands and shook his head, saying in a frustrated tone of voice, "I have no further questions of this witness."

The judge directed Mark to call his next witness.

Becky stepped forward and was sworn in.

Mark asked Becky, "What is your relationship to the defendant, ma'am?"

"I'm proud to say that I'm his wife and have been so honored to be for over sixteen years."

"Mrs. McDonald, you heard the previous witness testify that he saw your husband on the commuter train from the Pennsylvania Railroad Central Station on the evening of the twentieth of December, didn't you?"

"Yes I did."

"And did you have occasion to meet him that evening when the train stopped at the Westwood Station?"

"Yes, our four daughters and I met the train at six forty-seven as we usually do, and it was right on time, like always."

"You and Mr. McDonald have four daughters, don't you?"

"Yes we do and they're all beautiful young ladies who, like me, completely adore their daddy."

"Then what happened, Mrs. McDonald?"

"My husband, children, and I went to our daughter's basketball game over at the Pascack Hills High School in Woodcliff Lake."

"And what did you do after the game?"

"After we left our oldest daughter's basketball game, we had dinner together at the Saddle River Country Club, picked up our Christmas tree, and went home together."

"Did your husband leave you at any time during that evening?"

"No sir, he never left my sight at all. We both went to sleep at about eleven o'clock and he was arrested by a detective from the Bergen County Sheriff's office at a little after midnight."

"You heard the District Attorney claim that your husband had an affair with his assistant and murdered her. What is your response to that accusation?"

"It's the most absurd thing I have ever heard. My husband has always been kind, honest, and totally loyal to me, our four precious children, and to our marriage. He is the world's best husband to me and father to our children. The prosecutor obviously doesn't know my husband and seems to be more interested in getting himself re-elected by a dishonest conviction than he is in ensuring that justice is done in this case."

The DA stood up and angrily shouted, "Objection! The witness is only supposed to answer questions and not make such irrelevant and preposterous statements like she just did."

The judge replied, "Sustained. The witness will only answer questions posed to her and not make such statements."

Mark said, "Your witness."

The DA walked to the podium and asked, "Mrs. McDonald, do you love your husband enough that you would tell an outright lie if you believed it would save him from being convicted and incarcerated for the heinous crime for which he now stands accused?"

Mark shouted, "Objection, Your Honor. The District Attorney is posing a question to the witness that is ambiguous and hypothetical, and any answer she might give would generate a negative and confusing impression."

Judge Mattox said, "Sustained."

The DA then asked, "Mrs. McDonald, do you have a problem with alcohol?"

"Absolutely not. I do not drink."

"Have you ever experienced a drinking problem in the recent past?"

"No, I have not. Like I said, I don't drink."

The DA picked up a document, brought it to Becky, and asked if she recognized it. It was a copy of the summons that had been written for her DWI charge.

"Yes, I do. I don't know what this has to do with the issue at hand, sir, but it was a very foolish reaction I had to the stress caused by the highly unjust accusation of my husband. It was the first and only time in my entire life that I ever touched alcohol."

The DA shook his head, raised his arms into the air, and said, "So you say. I have no further questions of this obviously opinionated witness who, only a month ago was arrested and charged with driving while impaired, often referred to as drunk driving and has the nerve to lie before this court by claiming she doesn't drink."

Mark then stood up and said, "Your Honor, the prosecutor's last hostile and disrespectful remark was totally uncalled for and I request that the jury be directed to ignore it."

The judge then admonished the DA to not make such remarks and directed the jury to ignore the statement.

Mike leaned over to Mark and said, "I think we shouldn't put Wilson on the stand now. Let's stop it right here while the jury is obviously annoyed with the DA."

Mark nodded in agreement, then stood up and said, "Your Honor and members of the jury, the defense rests."

The judge then called for a recess until tomorrow when the prosecution and defense would present their closing arguments.

*   *   *

After wading through another crowd of Rev. Anton Jefferson's and Marcia Stone-Dunham's rabble rousers who were assembled in front of the courthouse each day of the trial, Wilson and Becky got into the rented chauffeur-driven limousine that would take them home, and Mark and Mike went to Mark's law office to prepare the defense's closing statement.

On their way home, Wilson raved over Becky's moving testimony, and told her that Mark and Mike said it was the strongest anyone could have given on his behalf . . . then Mark and Mike had agreed that Becky's moving testimony shouldn't be diluted with anything from the other few not nearly as impressive witnesses they had lined up to testify about lesser matters.

"I meant every word of what I said to that jerk DA, honey. I would kill anyone who would use you and our family for anything, and especially put your life on the line for his personal political gain, and that's exactly what the, pardon my language, bastard was doing."

Feeling confident that an acquittal was inevitably forthcoming, Wilson suggested that he and Becky go out for a nice dinner to celebrate what they and their attorneys sensed that the next day would bring; a positive end to the nightmare they had been experiencing for the past few months.

After dinner, they returned home and enjoyed a wonderful and sorely-needed "sleeping pill" together.

Early the next morning, they met Mike and Mark for breakfast at the diner before going over to the courthouse. Everyone was in a cheery and upbeat mood as Mark went over his closing argument and everyone seemed satisfied that it was perfect and right on target.

After breakfast, they headed across the street, through security, and into the courtroom.

After everyone was positioned, the bailiff announced, "All rise."

Judge Mattox entered and told everyone to be seated.

"Are the prosecution and defense prepared to give their closing statements?"

Both Mark and the DA responded in the affirmative.

The DA rose, slowly walked to the jury box, and said, "Ladies and gentlemen of the jury, you have heard several indisputable witnesses, including a certified expert from the Federal Bureau of Investigation, give testimony which clearly indicates that the defendant, James Wilson McDonald the third had the means, motive, and opportunity to brutally take the life of Miss Yolanda Lee Walker.

His car was seen by a witness at the location where her body was discovered, his fingerprints were on a bottle found on her body, evidence of an illicit affair between the deceased was found, and his only shallow defense was in the admittedly moving testimony of his wife who, like any good wife, would do or say anything to protect her husband, the testimony of a conductor who was serving hundreds of others that he saw him, and the grateful character testimony of a man who served with him many years ago . . . before he met the victim in this case.

The defense counsel referred to the evidence we presented to you against his client as 'circumstantial.' If it had been based on only one circumstantial item, we would not have even brought this case to trial . . . but it was several items, all interrelated and connecting, that painted the picture of what actually occurred. I therefore implore you to do your responsible duty and find the defendant guilty of murdering this innocent young lady and take his life from him as he did hers by sending him to prison for the remainder of his life. Thank you."

Mark then stood and said, "The prosecution has basically conceded from the very beginning of this trial that all . . . I said *all,* mind you . . . of its so-called evidence was purely circumstantial. You even heard most of the prosecution's witnesses use such terms as 'could have been, might have been,' and some possibilities were even weaker. The whiskey bottle had only one set of fingerprints. Mr. McDonald is not in the bottle manufacturing business so someone else had to have touched the bottle many times before it got into Mr. McDonald's hands . . . but strangely, only his fingerprints were on it. Why?

If someone wanted to make it appear that Mr. McDonald did what he's been unjustly accused of, they would get him to touch the bottle and then carefully protect the prints to ensure that he would be accused. I submit that this is exactly what happened . . . that someone had tried to frame him.

The ugly salacious cards that were found in Miss Walker's desk 'could have been' initialed by the defendant. *Could have been!* The truth is that Mr. McDonald did *not* place his easily forged initials on the disgusting cards.

The car that was seen the night before near where Miss Walker's body was found 'could have been' Mr. McDonald's . . . or one of several thousand other identical cars in the New York area. The witness couldn't even identify the driver's gender!

A distinguished college professor who served with him in a war to protect our country should have wiped out the unfounded allegations of racism that have been implied against him by the prosecution and our local news media. If there have been any acts of racism in this case, it's been from a very biased and uninformed media.

Two more reliable witnesses gave you sworn testimony that they saw Mr. McDonald at a time and place where he was nowhere near Miss Walker during the period the Medical Examiner stated that she was murdered. Yes, one of the witnesses was his dear wife to whom he has been loyal and faithful throughout their sixteen years of marriage. She knows the defendant better than any of us and made it perfectly clear that she believes in him and knows . . . *knows* . . . that he couldn't and wouldn't have done such a heinous thing as he's been unjustly accused of.

I therefore ask you ladies and gentlemen to perform your responsibilities as jurors and acquit Mr. McDonald so the law enforcement authorities may conduct more than the cursory investigation it has thus far conducted in this matter, and bring the *real* murderer of this young lady to justice. Thank you."

After Judge Mattox gave his instructions to the jury prior to their adjournment and said, "All parties to the trial will return at nine a.m. tomorrow or whenever the jury has reached its verdict. This court is now dismissed."

Mark, Mike, Wilson, and Becky packed up the defense documents and left the courthouse, feeling confident that the jury would surely be ruling for an acquittal early the next morning. After enjoying a pre-celebration dinner, they all exchanged "high-fives," all went home and retired for the evening. Glad that this nightmare appeared to be finally coming to a positive conclusion, Wilson and Becky then enjoyed one of their best ever "sleeping pills."

Chapter Eighteen

Early the following morning, just as the sun was rising, Wilson and Becky climbed out of bed, slipped into their sweat suits and tennis shoes, and went for a nice refreshing walk together through the wooded County Park behind their home.

As they walked hand in hand through the woods, Wilson said, "Honey, I'll be so happy to see this nightmare that we've all had to live through finally come to an end today. I feel that Mark and Mike really did do a bang-up job for us, especially in Mark's closing statement. And, if anything convinced the jury of my innocence, it had to be yours and Dr. Jackson's powerful, supporting testimonies. I thank you, my dear precious wife."

"No, don't thank me, Honey, because I meant every word of it, but I believe we should both thank our precious Lord for giving us each other. Let's kneel here together and offer Him our prayer of thanks."

They knelt together on the damp ground while holding hands, and offered a deep thanksgiving prayer; then returned home to prepare for their final journey of this nightmare into New York City. They hugged the girls prior to leaving and told them they would all go out to dinner together that evening to celebrate a good end to this nightmare.

Mike and Mark met them at the diner at 8:30 a.m. It was expected that the jury's verdict would probably come within the hour. At 10:45, Mark received a telephone call from the judge's office advising him that the jury had not yet reached a verdict, but they should remain on standby until one was reached. This threw a slight cloud over things, as everyone had believed an early verdict would surely be forthcoming.

Mike and Mark both knew from past experience that a delay in a jury's arriving at a verdict in a criminal case was often not a good sign, but didn't express such thoughts to Wilson and Becky. Rather than go all the way back to New Jersey and have to rush back again when the jury was ready, they agreed that they would just stay at the diner and chat and wait . . . and wait . . . and wait!

Finally, at a little after two p.m., Mark's cell phone rang, causing everyone at the table to jump. Mark listened and said, "Okay, we'll be right over."

"The jury has reached its verdict, so let's head across the street and get the good news."

After everyone was in the courtroom and seated, the jurors slowly filed in and took their seats in the jury box. Mike's experienced intuition caused him to sense the worst could be about to happen, based on the fact that it took the jury so long to reach a verdict and the glum look on the faces of the jurors as they entered the courtroom which all but confirmed it before a word was said. Judge Mattox then entered and everyone in the courtroom stood.

"Please be seated, ladies and gentlemen. Has the jury arrived at a verdict in the case of the State of New York versus James Wilson McDonald, III?"

The jury foreman slowly stood with a bowed head and said "We have Your Honor."

"Please state your findings."

The foreman said in a soft voice, "We the jury find the defendant, Mr. James Wilson McDonald the third *guilty* of murder in the first degree."

Becky let out a howling cry, and Wilson slammed his head down onto the table with his arms outstretched as Mike and Mark stood in stunned disbelief.

The judge then polled each individual juror and they all replied that they concurred with the finding. The judge then stated that the sentencing of McDonald would be scheduled in one week and quickly closed the court amidst cheers from many of the spectators and loud cries from some.

Three armed deputies quickly walked up to Wilson, handcuffed him, and led him out a side door where he was placed into a waiting van and taken directly back to his old temporary residence, a cell in the Manhattan House of Detention.

Mike and Mark had to nearly carry a hysterically crying Becky out of the court room and into the limousine that had been reserved for their anticipated victory ride back home. Instead of going directly back to the McDonald home, Mark directed the driver to take them to the Ridgewood Hospital. After Mark briefed Dr. Alexander, the on-duty psychiatrist of the situation, he gave her 30 milligrams of Valium and admitted her into the psychiatric unit on a suicide watch. Mark and Mike then went directly to the McDonald home.

When they arrived at the McDonald home, they found Wilson's daughters crying hysterically. A sobbing Elizabeth told them that the television news had said their daddy would probably be put in prison for the rest of his life. Mark and Mike tried to reassure them that the case would be appealed and was far from over yet, but this gave the girls little assurance. Mike decided that he would stay over at the home with the girls for the night.

*   *   *

Wilson sat alone in his cell at the Manhattan House of Detention, which was fully lighted and he was kept under observation, as he was also under a suicide watch. The prison's psychiatrist had loaded him up with several psychotropic medications which he was forced to take. Although he had been given enough drugs to put a herd of elephants to sleep, Wilson stayed wide awake in worry, not about himself, but about how Becky and the girls would be handling this devastating situation.

Back at the psychiatric unit in the New Jersey hospital where he was confined, Chester was elated when he saw the results of the trial on the television news, reacting to the trial's unexpected outcome as though he had won a great personal victory.

When they heard the bad news on television that afternoon, John and Diane DeBoer immediately jumped into their car and drove through the night up to New Jersey to be with Wilson's daughters who were struggling with the most severe form of anxiety imaginable, believing that they would never see their precious father again . . . regardless of everyone's efforts to convince them otherwise.

Many of Wilson's other friends, including his pastor, Reverend Ben, spent as much time as possible with the girls and in visiting a deeply hurting Becky at the hospital, who had to be medicated into a nearly comatose state.

After the DeBoer's arrived and the children were being taken care of, Mark and Mike went to the Manhattan House of Detention to see Wilson.

When he was brought into the attorney/client conference room, Wilson was surprisingly calmed, dry-eyed and nearly stoic. "Well, gentlemen, what's the next step? Do we stand the chance of a snowball in hell on an appeal? Please give it to me straight guys."

Mike replied, "To be frank with you, old friend, at this point we really don't have a lot to work with as far as possible trial errors go, even though I've never seen a more absurd jury conclusion; but you can be sure that we're going to attack it with everything we can. Our only hope as far as an appeal goes at this point is to find some major trial error or that Chester will either confess or some solid proof that he did it is discovered."

Wilson said, "To be honest with you, gentlemen, the way I view it is that the war is over and I have lost it, and I would prefer to take the death needle and get it over with as soon as possible than spend the rest of my life sitting in a prison cell. Fight for an overturn of the verdict, which we all know is a very long shot, but I don't want to exchange a quick and painless death for years of misery for both me and my family with my being in prison for the rest of my life. I also assume that Ms. Walker's family will probably be filing a civil action to take everything we have away from my family, so that doesn't leave me much to live for anyhow, does it?"

Mike replied, "Please don't give up yet, old friend, because we do have a fighting chance and, besides, there is no death penalty in New York State. We have both the appeal, where one never knows what might happen, and there's also a long shot chance that the real murderer, whom we all know was Chester, will be proven guilty. Remember, I had that happen several years ago in North Carolina and you can be sure that I'm not going to rest until the same thing happens here."

"Thanks Mike. I do appreciate what you're saying and I know you mean well, but let's be realistic about this. I'm not into criminal law like you and Mark are, but common sense tells me that Chester isn't going to confess to killing Yolanda, even if he's convicted of murdering his girlfriend . . . he's that kind of a low-living guy who'd allow me and my family to be destroyed before he'd do anything for me. Without a confession from him or some overwhelming proof that he did it, I'm simply done and am ready to deal with whatever comes."

Mike said, "Hey pal, we just might get ourselves that confession from Chester."

"And how do you propose that will happen?"

"I don't know yet, Wilson, but I haven't given up in our fight and neither should you. We will get that confession from him or somehow prove that that bastard, Chester, murdered Yolanda . . . and I'll bet my life on it. Try to hang in there, buddy, and I'll stop in and keep you posted every week until it happens."

Wilson sarcastically replied, "Sure Mike . . . sure."

Mark and Mike left, and Wilson was returned to his cell.

* * *

Becky finally came out of the haze the medications had put her in and asked to go home. Her psychiatrist was satisfied that although she was severely depressed, but was now rational and non-suicidal, and authorized her release. When she returned home, her girls rushed up to her and clung to her like paint. As far as they knew, she was all they had left because their beloved daddy was about to be put in prison for the rest of his life and they would never see him again.

Since Becky appeared to be growing a little more stable, John and Diane DeBoer decided they would stay for a couple of more days to be certain that she would be okay before they returned home to Fayetteville; but promised to be on standby for immediate recall if Becky needed their help.

* * *

Chester's mental condition was fully evaluated by the court appointed psychiatrist and he was found to be mentally capable of standing trial for the murder of Cassandra Lopez. A court appointed public defender would represent him at trial which was scheduled to take place the coming month.

Meanwhile, his employment at the firm had been terminated by his uncle, his car repossessed, his condominium foreclosed upon, and his law license indefinitely suspended. He had little to nothing left except the pleasure of knowing that he had destroyed his former boss and nemesis, Wilson, and his family. That was enough to satisfy his angry psychopathic and alcoholic personality.

He was incarcerated in the Bergen County Detention Center in Hackensack pending his trial, which was scheduled to take place in a month. While there, Chester was obsessed with the idea of finding a way to escape from the jail and spent his every waking minute studying the flow of activity around him to find it.

He hated being told what to do by the jail staff and having to contend with a regular diet of insults they fed him because he had been a lawyer. He observed and kept careful notes on every aspect of the security process . . . and then he finally discovered a way to make it happen!

He observed that on every Tuesday morning, the heating and air-conditioning contractor sent a technician in to check the jail's heating, ventilation, and air-conditioning system (HVAC), and the guy looked almost exactly like Chester . . . short, skinny, with a pencil-thin mustache and dark hair. His regular routine was to go into each cell to inspect the ducts for heating and cooling efficiency and to ensure that no contraband items had been slipped into the heating and air conditioning ducts by the inmates. He wore overalls and a base ball cap and was provided with a master key to unlock the cell doors, and was allowed free access within the building to do his work without any of the corrections staff observing him

On the morning of an HVAC inspection day, Chester feigned an illness, and the corrections medical technician allowed him to stay in his cell and rest. While the HVAC technician was in Chester's cell doing his regular inspection, Chester slipped up behind him and choked him until he was unconscious. After exchanging clothing with him, Chester quickly placed the man's body on his bunk and covered him with a blanket. He painted a thin mustache on his upper lip with a black magic marker he had earlier acquired and stashed, then picked up the technician's tool belt and headed for the door with his master key.

The guard on duty paid little attention as Chester casually walked by and waived at him and then opened the door leading to the alley where the technician's service van was parked. Chester slipped behind the wheel of the service van and quickly drove away from the building. His escape wasn't discovered for nearly an hour, during which time Chester had ditched the van and gotten himself a bottle of Crown Royal and a room in a cheap motel with money taken from the service technician's wallet.

In his motel room, Chester guzzled down his precious booze while he planned his final stab at Wilson, and decided that he would go after his family. In his angry, drunk, and irrational mind, he planned to rape Wilson's wife and kill her and their children. He thought, *After all, I can only be executed once so I might as well get them all and have myself a little fun while I'm doing it."*

*   *   *

As feared but not unexpected, Wilson was served with a civil complaint at the jail by Yolanda's parents' attorney, demanding one hundred million dollars for her death. When Mark and Mike came to see him, Wilson wadded up the document and threw the ball of paper at both of them saying, "Here's the final straw, gentlemen. It's all over now for me and my dear family. I'd welcome a death sentence now if they would offer me one since I really have nothing left to live for."

Mike explained that this civil action could not be executed until his appeal had been adjudicated, which they were in the process of filing, as well as preparing for his sentencing hearing scheduled for the coming week. But Wilson had obviously slipped way downhill in his mind, and the psychotropic drugs and lack of sleep were finally getting to him. He abruptly and angrily called for the guard who escorted him back to his cell without even saying goodbye to Mike and Mark.

As soon as he was back in his cell, Wilson crashed on his cot and immediately fell into a deep sleep. He then experienced another strange dream involving his mother and father's presence. Through a thick mental fog, he heard the voice of his father say, "Listen to me, son. You're not acting the way we taught you to do when faced with a difficult situation like the one you're in, so get with it boy."

His mother added, "You know how proud we've always been about you son, so please be that wonderful son that we love and stand up like the man we raised you to be."

His father then said, "When this crisis in your life passes, as I know it will, you want to be able to look back and feel proud of the way you've acted. Remember the football game against Duke back in the late eighties when everyone else had given up but you, and you charged forward and scored a last second touchdown . . . because you didn't give up. And, son, I hate to say it but right now you're not acting like that wonderful young man we were so proud of and loved. Then his father's voice kept echoing with, "this too shall pass, this too shall pass, etc. until he awakened and again wondered if he had actually experienced being with his parents in something other than a dream.

*   *   *

Becky, Mike, John, Diane, and the girls went to the Detention Center to visit Wilson. Mike had finally succeeded in convincing the girls that the final resolution of Wilson's situation was a long way off. He and Mark had meticulously gone over the trial record, word by word, and letter by letter. They picked up several possible trial errors, especially in the Judge's instructions to the jury and Chester's unannounced appearance, which he felt could result in the appellate court's ruling it a mistrial.

As a result of Wilson's surreal dream, his entire attitude suddenly took a strong turn uphill. He was cheerful and upbeat during his visit with his family and friends, and was again the Wilson of old. Even Becky and the children were uplifted by Wilson's positive cordiality and smiling face. The corrections officer supervising their visit even turned her head away so they could all hug Wilson.

CHAPTER NINETEEN

On the day after his escape from jail, Chester stole an automobile from the parking lot of the motel he was in and drove to the park behind Wilson's Saddle River home, then hid in the woods directly behind the home in a position where he could get a good view of what was going on around the house. When he saw Becky and the children leave as she drove them to school, he slipped up closer to the house and positioned himself flat on the ground in a clump of bushes beside the garage and awaited Becky's return.

About fifteen minutes later, her van pulled into the driveway and Chester crouched low until the automatic garage door opened, then slipped inside behind her van unnoticed while she was parking and before she closed the garage door.

As Becky walked to the door from the garage, Chester slipped in behind her, put a chokehold on her neck and pressed a knife firmly against her throat.

"Listen to me you bitch and do what I tell you to or you're dead. Get inside the house so you and I can do what

I know you've wanted me to do to you since I was in your house last year. I'm gonna screw you like your husband tried to screw me, but ours is gonna be more fun."

Becky begged, "Let me go, Chester. Please let me go."

"No way, and if you fight me you'll regret it . . . so let's you and me head for your bedroom right now and get it on. I've been waiting to do this for a long time."

* * *

John and Diane had left the McDonald home earlier that morning and decided to stop for breakfast at a local diner before heading back to Fayetteville. After breakfast, they saw an antique store across the street and stopped in to check out their inventory since antique collecting was an interest they shared.

They found an old oil painting on sale that interested them. John made a lowball offer on it, which the store owner accepted. When he opened his wallet to take out his credit card and pay for it, he realized that he had left it at Wilson's home when he made a purchase on the internet the evening before. Since they were only about twenty miles away from Wilson's home and Becky had given him a key to the house, they decided to drive back and retrieve the credit card rather than bother asking Becky to mail it.

* * *

Becky kept pleading with Chester to leave her alone, promising that she wouldn't tell anyone about his assault of her if he would.

"No way, bitch, now take off your clothes and let me see that sexy body or I'll send you to the same place where I sent those other bitches when they pissed me off."

Becky pleadingly asked again, "Please let me go, Chester, and I swear to you that I won't tell anyone."

Unknown to Chester, their conversation and activities were being videotaped on a monitoring system which Wilson had installed for security and Becky activated it when she pushed a button beside the light switch as they entered the bedroom.

Chester grinned and said, "You think I'm stupid, don't you? You'll call the cops the second I leave here so I'm afraid you're gonna have to be joining Cassandra and that other bitch, Yolanda, after I get through doing you. They lied to me too and I had to kill both of them. Sorry Becky, but at least when I'm finished with doing you, you're gonna die a mighty happy woman. I can promise you that much!"

Aware that Chester would probably soon kill her, Becky decided she would try to make something positive out of this situation. She sighed and said, "Okay, Chester. I won't fight you; in fact, if you'll tell me a couple of things that I've been wondering about since you're going to kill me anyhow, I won't struggle and I'll even try to make what you're wanting to do to me more enjoyable for you.

"Hmm, that sounds like an invitation that'll be hard to refuse. What do you want me to tell you about?"

"Like how and why did you kill Yolanda Walker?"

"Hmmm . . . I guess it won't hurt to tell you now since you're gonna die soon anyhow; that is if you promise me that you'll really give me a good time in bed before I kill you."

"I promise you I will, Chester; I'll give you the very best time of your life and do anything you want me to."

"Okay, I saw her standing in front of our building on Wall Street one afternoon a few days before Christmas. She was trying to catch a taxi to take her to the airport and was having trouble finding one, so I volunteered to drive her there in my car. She's the no-good lying bitch who accused me of touching her boobs in the elevator and told your bastard of a husband, who then humiliated me about it in front of my sonofabitch uncle and I damned near got fired for it."

"I don't blame you for feeling angry towards him, Chester, even if he is my husband, because he shouldn't have done something that mean to you."

"Well, at least I don't have to worry about him anymore because he's gonna get what he deserves when they send him to the slammer for the rest of his life for what he did to me."

"Tell me what happened after Yolanda got into your car, Chester? You promised me you would tell me everything, and I know you're a man of your word."

"I drove her past the LaGuardia Airport and asked if she wanted to stop and have a drink with me somewhere before I dropped her off. She started getting nasty with me, and accusing me of stuff I didn't do. She demanded that I turn around and go back to the airport or let her out right there on the parkway. I just rubbed her leg a little and she slapped my hand and started screaming insults at me. I told her to shut the hell up, but she started screaming louder so I hit her hard in the mouth. She screamed more, so I pulled off of the parkway and stopped. She screamed even louder, so I picked up a flat rock that was beside the road and hit her with it until she stopped screaming . . . and when she finally did shut up she was dead."

Sounding sympathetic, Becky replied, "Goodness, Chester, I'm sorry you had to go through so much that wasn't really your fault. She shouldn't have treated you that way."

"Thank you for understanding, Becky. It was terrible, so I just put her body in the car trunk while I got something to drink to calm my nerves, and then took her to my home over in New Jersey. Then I took her body back to New York later that night and left her in an alleyway near the office."

"Well why do you think the police charged Wilson for doing it?" Becky asked.

"That was the best part of all as far as I'm concerned. He'd done me real wrong by embarrassing me more times than I can tell you about that and lots of other things, so I figured it was my chance to pay him for all he'd done to hurt me. So my girlfriend and I put the stuff in his office and I took a bottle of scotch whiskey that one of our clients had handed him, wrapped it in cloth, and jammed it in the bitch's stiff hand. Pretty smooth plan, huh? Now let's you and I have that good time that you promised me we'd have after I told you what really happened."

"Do you swear to me that everything you told me is the absolute truth, Chester? That you really did kill that girl, Yolanda."

With a wide grin, Chester said, "Cross my heart, baby . . . I sure as hell did and I planned the whole thing all by myself! Now come on and give me some of the good stuff that you promised me."

As Chester and Becky were talking, John and Diane pulled into the McDonald driveway, walked up the walkway and entered the front door. He shouted up the stairs, "Anybody home?"

When Becky heard John's voice downstairs, she screamed loudly, "Help me, John! I'm upstairs in my bedroom. Please help me!"

John and Diane raced up the stairs and entered Becky's bedroom where Chester stood naked and frozen in shock. With no hesitation, John raced towards Chester and hit him squarely in the jaw, knocking him down on the floor. Chester got up and picked up his knife from the table and lunged at John, barely scraping him on the thigh. He pulled back and came towards John again with the knife pointed at his face.

As John and Chester were fighting for the knife, Becky quickly moved behind Chester with a heavy wrought iron lamp in her hand and brought it crashing down on his head, knocking him completely unconscious.

Becky hugged John and Diane and tearfully said, "Thank God you two wonderful people came back when you did. You saved my life because he was going to rape and kill me afterwards. And guess what, my dear friends? I have his confession for killing Yolanda Walker captured on videotape!" John and Diane were delighted to hear that news.

John tied Chester up with a few extension cords and duct tape, and called the police who arrived in a few minutes and dragged a now conscious, hurting and very angry Chester away in handcuffs.

The telephone rang and it was Elizabeth. "Mom, we've been waiting for you in front of the school for nearly a half hour. Why aren't you here to get us?"

Becky happily replied, "Because, my dear, your daddy is going to be freed from jail and will be coming home to us soon, and I'm busy taking care of it. Stay there and I'll come get you in a few minutes."

When Elizabeth told her sisters the good news they were elated. She told Becky to take care of that more important business and they would be glad to walk the three miles home. They skipped the whole way home, deliriously happy over the news that their daddy would be coming back to them!

Becky called the company that had installed the security system so they could ensure that the videotape was properly removed and not in any way disturbed. She then called Mike and Mark, who were also ecstatic over this great news and came rushing to the home.

After the girls came home, they, Mark, Mike, John, Diane, and Becky raced over to the Detention Center to share the good news with Wilson. Everyone hugged and deliriously danced around the visitor's room like crazed people!

*   *   *

The following morning, Mark took a copy of the videotape to the New York District Attorney's office. The DA was clearly negative and disappointed, and initially tried to object to it, taking the shallow position that Chester's confession was taken under false pretenses and the chain of possession of the tape wasn't managed according to procedure, and shouldn't be admissible. When it was shown to Judge Mattox, he took the opposite position and ordered that Wilson be acquitted and immediately released from the Detention Center.

There were several time-consuming legal and administrative procedures that had to be taken care of for his release and to clear the charges against Wilson . . . then formally charge Chester with Yolanda's murder. With Mike and Mark's diligent help, the procedures were expedited and completed in a record five days, and Wilson was free at last!

*　　*　　*

When Wilson was finally released from the Detention Center he was driven home in a limousine with Becky and the girls, who clung closely to him and showered him with loving hugs and kisses all the way home.

To Wilson's pleasant surprise, his homecoming had become a major news event, and nearly everyone in his church and many old friends from Fayetteville had been invited by Becky to come up for the occasion to welcome him home. The large crowd of well over a hundred people was gathered in his yard cheering Wilson as the car carrying him and his family pulled into the driveway.

Even the rabble-rouser, Rev. Anton Jefferson, and the angry feminist, Marcia Stone-Dunham, were present for the event at the advice of their lawyers to publicly apologize for their previous actions against Wilson, mainly to protect themselves from future law suits.

When Wilson reached out to shake Jefferson's hand, Becky stepped between them and kicked Anton solidly in the groin, gave Marcia Stone-Dunham a "bitch-slap" that could be heard a block away, and then waved to the cheering crowd

After exchanging hugs and handshakes with many of the gathered welcoming group, he was interviewed by the now-supportive local ABC television station and asked how he felt about the outcome.

Wilson's response to the reporter's question: "I want to thank you, my dear friends, for sharing this wonderful day with me. As my Lord, my family, and my friends have tried to assure me all along about every negative thing that happens in our lives, I now know they were right when they said to me that **this too shall pass.** I am indeed a very blessed man . . ."

Some major events that will follow:

- Chester will be convicted of the murders of Cassandra and Yolanda, and receive two consecutive life sentences in the New Jersey and New York prison systems with no chance of parole . . . but he will never be able to serve either sentence because he will be stabbed to death by another inmate in his first year of incarceration at New Jersey's Rahway Prison.
- The New York District Attorney will be publicly chastised for his handling of Wilson's case and not be re-elected.
- Wilson's law license will be restored and he will later be elected to serve as a District Court Judge in Cumberland County, North Carolina, later followed by an appointment as a Justice on the North Carolina State Supreme Court.

- Becky and Wilson will purchase the Fayetteville home in which he was raised to be their permanent earthly residence and love nest.
- Wilson and Becky will have one more child, a son, whom they will name Michael. Dr. Deshawn Jackson, Mike Williford, and Dr. John DeBoer will be asked and proudly accept to serve as Michael's co-godfathers.
- Becky will earn her Ph.D. degree in Psychology from Duke University and open her own clinic in Fayetteville, which specializes in the counseling of troubled adolescent girls.
- Elizabeth will receive a basketball scholarship to the University of North Carolina, from which she will graduate with honors, and serve as a high school math teacher and girls' basketball coach at the Fayetteville Academy. She will also star in several musicals at the Cape Fear Regional Theatre.
- Taylor will earn a bachelor's degree in Fine Arts from St. Mary's University and become a widely acclaimed artist. She will also publish a best-selling novel that will be made into a major movie. She will marry a Fayetteville dentist and they will have beautiful twin girls.
- Sarah will earn a degree in journalism from the University of South Carolina, became a popular national talk show host on Fox News, marry a major sports celebrity, and later be elected to serve in the

United States Congress. Sarah and her husband will have two girls and two boys.

- Lauren will graduate from the Julliard School of Music in New York, and perform as a highly successful ballet dancer and opera singer. She and her opera star husband will have two beautiful daughters.
- Wilson's cousin, Warren, with whom he served in the Army, will earn his Ph.D. and become a department chair at the Methodist University in Fayetteville.
- Michael will become an honors student at Terry Sanford High School in Fayetteville where he will star on the football, baseball, and basketball teams just as his father did.

IF

by Rudyard Kipling

If you can keep your head when all about you,
    Are losing theirs and blaming it on you;
If you can trust yourself when all men doubt you,
    But make allowance for their doubting too:
If you can wait and not be tired by waiting,
    Or, being lied about, don't deal in lies,
Or being hated don't give way to hating,
    And yet don't look too good, nor talk too wise;

If you can dream—and not make dreams your master;
    If you can think—and not make thoughts
    your aim;
If you can meet with Triumph and Disaster
    And treat those two imposters just the same:
If you can bear to hear the truth you've spoken
    Twisted by knaves to make a trap for fools,
Or watch the things you gave your life to, broken,
    And stoop and build 'em up with work-out tools;

If you can make one heap of all your winnings
    And risk it on one turn of pitch-and-toss,
And lose, and start again at your beginnings,
    And never breathe a word about your loss:
If you can force your heart and nerve and sinew
    To serve your turn long after they are gone,
And so hold on when there is nothing let in you
    Except the Will which says to them: "Hold on!"

If you can talk with crowds and keep your virtue,
    Or walk with Kings—nor lose the common touch,
If neither foes nor loving friends can hurt you,
    If all men count with you, but none too much:
If you can fill the unforgiving minute
    With sixty seconds' worth of distance run,
Yours is the Earth and everything that's in it,
    And—which is more—you'll be a Man, my son!

Dear Reader,

When the inevitable dark days come into your life, just as they did in Wilson's, remember that they too shall pass . . . IF you keep faith in the caring love of Him who created you and confidence in yourself. It has worked wonderfully for me in my life!

Edward Vaughn

ww.edwardvaughn.com

And always remember . . .

When things don't look so cheerful,
Just show a little fight.
For every bit of darkness,
There's a little bit of light.
For every bit of hatred,
There's a little bit of love.
And for every cloudy morning,
There's a midnight moon above.